Woven
Threads

Judith McCoy Miller

Heartsong Presents

Dedicated to my husband, Jim, for giving me the wonderful opportunity to become one of the threads woven into the fabric of his life, and in memory of our daughter, Michelle, with whom we shall be rewoven in heaven.

A note from the author:
I love to hear from my readers! You may write to me at the following address: **Judith McCoy Miller**
Author Relations
P.O. Box 719
Uhrichsville, OH 44683

ISBN 1-57748-196-8

WOVEN THREADS

Cover illustration by Kathy Arbuckle.

PRINTED IN THE U S A

Dr. Tessie Wilshire is about to start her life as a doctor for the Santa Fe Railroad.

"I think I just may be able to force myself to practice medicine here," Tessie answered with a grin that made her appear much younger than her twenty-eight years.

"If you think you know your way around the place well enough, I better get back to the train station. I've got some paperwork to take care of before going back to the hotel," Charlie told her, not wanting to leave but realizing she was weary.

"I'll be just fine. I plan to make an early night of it," she said, walking with him toward the front door.

"Please say you'll have breakfast with me," he requested as they reached the porch, not wanting to distance himself from her until he was sure when he would see her again.

"Since I've nothing here to eat, how could I turn down such an invitation?" she answered, regretting immediately how coquettish she sounded.

Taking her hand, he lifted it to his lips and gently placed a kiss on her palm. "Until morning," he said, smiling.

Tessie watched Charlie as he walked down the sidewalk toward the train station and then she sat down on the porch step. . .

"Thank You, Lord. I don't know what plans You have for me in this place, but thank You for sending me here," she whispered.

JUDITH MCCOY MILLER makes her home with her family in Kansas. *Threads of Love* was her first inspirational romance novel, and it was very popular with readers.

Books by Judith McCoy Miller

HEARTSONG PRESENTS
HP223—Threads of Love

Charlie Banion stared down at the list of names scribbled on his calendar; Mary had scheduled five interviews starting at one o'clock. Allowing a half-hour for each, he could still catch the four o'clock train and be in Florence for dinner. Hopefully this group would be better than the last. He had been at this three days now and still hadn't met the quota he needed for the remaining railroad jobs. No doubt the boss was going to be unhappy with his lack of success.

Might as well get a bite to eat before I start again, he thought, wishing the afternoon was already behind him. Tapping his pencil on the large wooden desk, he leaned back in his chair and wondered why it had been so difficult to find the employees he was looking for this time. It was easy enough locating general laborers to lay track, but now they needed some good reliable men with mechanical skills to keep the trains running. His attempt to find the caliber of employees they were looking for had gone lacking, especially when the applicants were told they would have to relocate to smaller towns.

"Sitting here thinking about it, isn't going to accomplish anything," he mumbled to himself, walking toward the office door.

"I'll be back in time for my one o'clock appointment, Mary," he said, striding past the secretary's desk.

"Yes, sir, I'll put the file on your desk," she answered. He didn't even glance her way as he nodded his head up and down in affirmation.

"Isn't he the most handsome thing you've ever seen?"

Mary inquired of the short, round brunette sitting at the desk across the room.

"I guess. That is, if you like single men who are six feet tall with broad shoulders, wavy black hair, and slate gray eyes," she answered, both of them giggling at her response.

"He doesn't seem to notice me at all," Mary complained, "even though I take forever primping for work when I know he'll be around."

"Maybe he's got a gal at one of the other stations, or back east somewhere," Cora volunteered, aware that most men found it difficult to overlook Mary Wilson, even when she didn't primp for hours.

"I'd even be willing to share him with one of those eastern society women. At least until I get him hooked," Mary responded, pushing back from her desk. "Guess I'll go to lunch, too. Maybe I can find a seat next to Mr. Banion. Keep an eye on things until I get back," she ordered Cora who sat looking after her with a look of envy and admiration etched on her face.

&

Tessie Wilshire stared out the window of the clacking train, unable to keep her mind from racing. The newly bloomed columbine and wild flax were poking their blossoms toward the sun after a long cold winter. Fields of winter wheat appeared in shades of bright green giving the countryside the appearance of a huge well-manicured lawn.

In about three months this will be a sea of golden yellow ready for the threshers and harvest crews, she thought. She had forgotten the beauty of these wheat fields and the Kansas prairie. It was hard to believe she had been gone so long and yet, things hadn't changed so very much. *I've missed it more than I realized,* she mused, trying to keep herself from thinking about the upcoming interview.

Always a pretty child, Tessie's age had enhanced her

beauty even more. The red hair of her youth had turned a deep coppery shade and the freckles of her childhood had finally given way to a flawless creamy complexion. Her bright blue eyes were accented by long golden lashes and her full lips turned slightly upward, punctuated by a small dimple at each side.

"Topeka. Next stop Topeka," came the conductor's call as he made his way down the narrow aisle between the seated passengers.

Tessie felt herself stiffen at the announcement. In an effort to relax, she took a deep breath and said softly, "I'm going to be fine. I know this is where God wants me."

"Watch your step, miss," the conductor instructed, extending his hand to assist Tessie as she stepped down from the train.

"Thank you. Could you tell me where I might find Mr. Banion's office?" she inquired, pulling on her gloves.

"He would be in the stationmaster's office, miss. Just go in the main door and turn to your right," he replied, thinking it had been a long time since he had since such a beauty.

Tessie clicked open the small brooch pinned to her lapel. The timepiece hidden inside revealed she had only a few moments to spare. Quickening her step, she turned and walked toward the office identified by the conductor.

❧

"Is the last one here yet, Mary?" Charlie Banion called from the station master's office.

"Haven't seen anyone. You want me to show him in when he gets here?" she asked, posing against the doorway to his office in an effort to gain his attention.

"That'll be fine," he answered, not looking in her direction. *Only one more left,* he thought, *and I'll be out of here.* At least the afternoon hadn't been a total waste. He had hired three of the last four applicants. If they didn't need a doctor so badly at the Florence train yard, he would be tempted to call it a day.

❧

Seeing the look of frustration on Mary's face as she returned to her desk, Cora shrugged her shoulders at the other woman. "Maybe he's not feeling well," she offered.

"Right!" came Mary's sarcastic response as she plopped down in her chair and watched a beautiful redhead walking toward the door.

"Good afternoon, I'm Tessie Wilshire. I believe Mr. Banion is expecting me at three o'clock," she announced, glancing from Mary to Cora, not sure which one was in charge.

"Don't think so. The Harvey Girls are interviewed next door in the restaurant office," Mary answered in an aloof tone.

"I'm not sure what a Harvey Girl is, but my appointment is with Mr. Charles Banion for three o'clock. I received a letter over a month ago scheduling this appointment," Tessie replied, fearing there had been a mix-up and she had traveled to Topeka for nothing.

"Mr. Banion doesn't interview for Mr. Harvey. I don't think they're even taking applications right now. The new women finished training yesterday and they're leaving on the next train," Mary advised haughtily, irritated by the woman's persistence.

"I'm trying to explain to you that my appointment is with Mr. Banion. I have never heard of Mr. Harvey," Tessie said, trying to hold her temper, but wishing she could shake some sense into the secretary's head.

Hearing the commotion in the outer office, Charlie walked to the doorway. "What seems to be the problem, Mary?" he asked, locking eyes with the gorgeous redhead standing in front of the secretary's desk.

"She says she has an appointment with you, Mr. Banion. I told her the Harvey Girls are interviewed next door but she won't listen. Keeps insisting she's to meet with you," his secretary answered, her exasperation obvious.

"Mr. Banion," Tessie said, extending her hand, "I am Dr. Wilshire and I believe we have a three o'clock appointment."

"Indeed we do Miss. . .uh, Dr. Wilshire, please come in," he replied, ushering her into his office and then turning to give Mary a glare.

"I didn't know. . . ," came the secretary's feeble reply, as the door closed behind them. She slowly slid down into her chair, her jaw gone slack in astonishment at the tı rn of events.

"How was I supposed to know?" she hissed at Cora.

"It'll be all right. He'll understand. Anybody could have made the same mistake," Cora replied, attempting to cheer her friend.

❧

"Have a seat, Dr. Wilshire," Charlie offered, moving to the other side of the desk. "I must admit, I'm as surprised as my secretary. I didn't realize you were a woman. . .well, I mean I realize you're a woman but I didn't know. . . ," he stammered.

"It's quite all right, Mr. Banion. I gather you've not studied my application," she said, giving him a bright smile that caused his heart to skip a beat.

"To be honest, I've been conducting interviews for several days now and I must admit I didn't look at any of the files for today's interviews," he responded, somewhat embarrassed by his lack of preparation. "I usually don't take such a lackadaisical attitude, but interviewing is not a job I particularly enjoy. After several days, it loses absolutely all appeal," he continued, in an attempt to redeem himself.

"I'm sure it can become quite tiring," she stated. "Of course, for those of us being interviewed, it's a very important appointment," she said, a hint of criticism edging through her soft tone.

"I realize that and I do apologize. If I'd done my homework, it would have saved everyone needless discomfort," he answered, flipping open her application file.

"I can assure you Mr. Vance is aware I'm not a man. I met him on one of his visits to Chicago and we've written on several occasions. When he discovered I was from Kansas, he encouraged me to apply for this position," she responded, realizing Mr. Banion was flustered and somewhat embarrassed by the whole scenario.

"So you've already met the president of the Santa Fe, Mr. Vance. He's always on the lookout for capable employees," Charlie replied.

Watching as he hastily read through her file, Tessie settled back in the overstuffed chair. Although the office decor was masculine, it was an inviting room. The large desk was of a rich mahogany with matching chair. A table along the north wall was ornately carved from the same wood and held several stacks of papers and files, the only visage of disarray throughout the office. Oil paintings in ornate gilded frames were tastefully displayed on several walls. Tessie noticed a picture of Mr. Vance and several austere looking gentlemen standing in front of a locomotive. In the picture, Mr. Vance appeared somewhat younger and much more pompous than the man she had met in Chicago.

"It seems your application is in order and I have only a few questions, Dr. Wilshire," Charlie commented, startling Tessie who had become absorbed in her surroundings. "Sorry, I didn't mean to alarm you," he said, noting she had jumped at the sound of his voice.

"I must have been daydreaming. The trip was more tiring

than I anticipated," she responded, bringing her eyes directly forward to meet his. "What questions did you wish to ask me?" she inquired with great formality.

"I have a list of specific questions I ask the men applying for positions with the railroad, but I don't think those would apply to you," he said with a smile, hoping to ease the procedure. "Why are you interested in working for the railroad?" he asked.

"I believe it's where God wants me to practice medicine," she quickly responded, sitting so straight she appeared to have a rod down her back.

"Well, that's one I've not heard before. I've been told it's where someone's wife or mother wants them to work, but I've never heard the railroad being where God wanted anyone," he said, with a chuckle.

"You needn't laugh at me, Mr. Banion," Tessie retorted, her cheeks turning flush and her back becoming even more rigid.

"I'm not laughing at you, Dr. Wilshire, and I'm not doubting the honesty of your statement. If you say God wants you with the Santa Fe Railroad, who am I to argue? Besides, your file reflects the necessary credentials and a letter of recommendation from Mr. Vance. There's really nothing for me to do except tell you the job is yours if you want it," he said, hoping to complete the interview without making her an enemy.

"Since you've offered the position, I have a few questions for you, Mr. Banion," she responded, her voice lacking much warmth.

"Please, call me Charlie," he requested. "I'll be glad to answer any questions, if you'll grant that one concession," he said giving her a beseeching look.

"Fine," she responded. "I need to know when I am to report for the position, what the living accommodations are in the community and, of course, what my salary will be," she answered without using his name in any form.

"Well, Tessie. . .may I call you Tessie since you've agreed to call me Charlie?" he asked, watching for her reaction.

"That will be fine," she replied, not meeting his eyes.

"Good, because we'll probably be seeing quite a bit of each other and I much prefer being on a first name basis with people. I don't hold much stock in. . ."

"Mr. Banion. . .Charlie, I've agreed we'll be on a first name basis if I accept the position. If you'll answer my questions, I'll be able to decide if I want to accept the offer," she interrupted.

"You told me God wants you working for the Santa Fe, Tessie, and I've offered you that opportunity. You can hardly turn it down, can you?" he said with a grin. "Oh, all right, I'll answer your questions," he continued, seeing that she was becoming exasperated with him. "The position begins immediately. You can catch the four o'clock train if I'm through answering your questions by then. If not, you'll have to catch the ten o'clock. The salary is $150 a month and the railroad furnishes your house. No choice on the house, it belongs to the railroad."

"You don't really expect me to begin today, do you?" she queried, her eyes wide in disbelief.

"Yes, I thought you understood that when a position was offered, employment was immediate. Isn't that what your letter stated?"

"Well, yes, but I didn't think it—I suppose I should have made arrangements," she stated, her voice full of hesitation.

"Are you accepting the position, Dr. Wilshire?" Charlie inquired with some of the formality she had exhibited earlier.

"Yes, but I'll need to make arrangements to have my belongings sent if I must start immediately," she answered, hoping he would grant some leniency.

"It's not my rule. I'd allow you as much time as you need, but it's a rule enforced for all new employees. There's no problem about your belongings, though. The railroad will ship them for you free of charge. Just a little added benefit," he remarked, not sure she was convinced he couldn't bend the rule.

"We have about thirty minutes before the train leaves. Have you had a chance to eat?" he asked.

"No, but I'm not hungry," she answered. "I'll wait until I get to Florence."

"Well, in that case, perhaps you'll join me for dinner?"

"You're going to Florence?" she queried.

"Sure am. I'm the operations manager which means I spend a lot of time there keeping things on schedule, so you'll be seeing a lot of me," he responded with a grin, hoping she would be pleased.

"I'll need to purchase a ticket and send word to my family that I've accepted the position. Since you're going to Florence, I suppose you'll be available to answer any other inquiry I might have," she said with a question in her voice.

"You can be assured I will make myself available to you whenever and wherever you request," he answered, his gray eyes twinkling.

She wasn't sure if he was making fun of her and decided it wasn't important enough to bother with. "If the interview is over, Mr. Banion," she began, rising from the chair.

"Charlie, remember you said you'd call me Charlie," he reminded, coming around the side of the desk. "As far as I'm concerned the interview is over, but you need not rush to buy a ticket. Your travel on the railroad is free. Another benefit of the job," he said, escorting her to the door.

"May I at least buy you a cup of coffee after you've sent your message home?" he invited as they walked through the outer office.

"I suppose that would be acceptable," she replied, her voice lacking much enthusiasm at the prospect.

"I'll meet you next door at the Harvey House when you've finished," he responded.

Had he not been looking at her back and observed the slight nod of her head, he wouldn't have known she even heard him speak. Staring after her as she walked across the room, he was unable to remember when he had been quite so impressed with a young woman.

"Did you have any letters you needed to take care of?" Mary asked, attempting to regain Charlie's attention.

"What? Oh, yes, I need to get a letter written to Mr. Vance advising him of the new employees I've hired," he responded.

When he had finished dictating the letter, Mary's worst fears were confirmed. He had hired the stunning redhead and the possibility of snagging a marriage proposal out of Charlie Banion was going to be more difficult that she had anticipated.

"I'd like that ready for my signature before the train leaves. I'm going to the restaurant but I'll return to sign it shortly," he instructed Mary and hurried toward the lunch counter, anxious to once again be in the company of the newest employee of the Santa Fe Railroad.

two

Tessie had just finished a cup of tea when Charlie arrived in the restaurant and seated himself opposite her. "Sorry to have taken so long. I had to get a letter dictated to Mr. Vance," he explained, feeling like a schoolboy on a first date.

"No need to apologize. I'm quite used to taking care of myself," she told him as the waitress brought Charlie a cup of coffee. "Living alone while in college and medical school has tended to make me quite independent. I've learned to use time alone quite constructively."

Before Charlie could decide if she had dubbed him a welcome intrusion or a pesky annoyance, the conductor's shout rang out, "All aboard."

"I've got to go back to the office for a few minutes. I'll see you on board," he said, getting up from his seat.

"Fine," Tessie answered nonchalantly, more interested in the group of chattering young women anxiously waiting on the platform. She wondered who they were and why they were all boarding a train to some tiny town seventy-five miles to the southwest. Picking up her black medical bag, she mentally gave thanks that Uncle Jon had insisted she carry it. "Never know when you might happen upon an emergency. If you're a doctor you ought to be prepared. Preachers carry a Bible and doctors ought to carry the tools of their trade too," he had counseled.

He and Aunt Phiney had given her sound advice thus far. They had warned she should pack a few personal belongings in case the train was delayed or the interview postponed, requiring her to be away more than one day.

Because of their foresight, she would at least have a few clothes until her trunks arrived.

The young women were seated on the train by the time Tessie boarded. Picking her way down the aisle, she found an empty seat, settled herself, and placed her bag on the floor. Just as the train began its lumbering exit from the station, Charlie bounded down the aisle and slid onto the seat across the aisle from her.

"Were you worried I wouldn't make it?" he inquired, a smile spread across his face.

"To be honest, my thoughts were occupied with all these young women, wondering where they come from and why they left their homes," she responded, not realizing such a remark was a rarity to a man of Charlie Banion's looks and position.

"You sure know how to keep a man from feeling sure of himself, don't you?" he asked, jokingly.

"What? Oh, I'm sorry, what were you saying? Isn't she a beautiful child?" Tessie inquired, nodding toward the little girl sitting on the seat in front of her.

Charlie broke forth in a laugh, aware that he would not engage this lovely woman in any meaningful conversation until she had surveyed all the passengers. "She is a pretty child," he answered, looking at the youngster and smiling into the small dark brown eyes that were staring back at him. The child's eyes quickly darted back toward Tessie.

"Hello, my name is Tessie," she said to the young girl. "What's your name?"

The child smiled and turned around facing them. She perched on her knees resting her arms across the back of the seat. "Hi, I'm Addie Baker. That's my sister, Lydia," she answered, pointing across the aisle toward the front of the train, her words slightly garbled. The gesture caught her sister's eye.

"Addie, turn around and mind your business," Lydia reprimanded the youngster, her lips mouthing the words in exaggerated fashion, although her voice was but a whisper. The child nodded, immediately turned and stared out the window, only to be met by her own forlorn reflection in the glass.

Tessie leaned forward and whispered, "I'm pleased to meet you, Addie," but the child gave no response and Tessie received a sharp look from the older sister.

Charlie turned his legs toward the aisle and leaned forward, resting his arms on his thighs. "I'd be happy to visit with you."

Tessie was tempted to ignore his forward behavior but allowed her interest in the young women to take precedence over Charlie's obvious lack of manners.

"Tell me about these young women. I believe you called them Harvey Girls," she requested, pulling off her gloves and reaching to remove a pearl hat pin from the navy blue adornment perched on her head.

He didn't answer for a moment but watched her movements, totally entranced by the feminine display. When she finally looked at him to see if he had heard the question, he smiled. "I'd rather talk about you but if that's not your choice of subject, I'll tell you a little about the Harvey Girls."

He remained seated with his legs in the aisle allowing him closer proximity to her. "These women have just completed their training as Harvey Girls and are going to work at the Harvey House in Florence. It's a hotel and restaurant, close to the train station. Fred Harvey has a contract with the Santa Fe railroad to place restaurants near some of the train stations. The one in Topeka is merely a restaurant, a very good one I might add, but Fred decided a hotel and restaurant would be even better at some of the stations."

"Are these women hired as maids for the hotel?" she interrupted, her interest peaked.

"Some of them may end up doing that part of the time," he responded, "but primarily they are hired and trained to work as waitresses in the restaurants. Fred has extremely high standards and the women must live in the establishment. Even in Topeka, those who work for him must reside in the accommodations he provides."

"Even if their parents live in the same town?" she asked, entranced with the idea.

"Yes, even then. It's one of the hard and fast rules of the Harvey Houses, just like our hard and fast rule that you begin work immediately," he replied, hoping she would indicate her forgiveness.

"From the size of the group, it looks like there are plenty of women interested in the jobs," she observed, once again scrutinizing the young women clustered at the front of the coach and ignoring his remark about rules.

"Fred pays a decent wage and for many of these women, it's the only opportunity they'll have to see a bit of the country. It's exciting for many of them and they're hoping for a better life than they've come from would be my guess," he stated, staring at her long graceful fingers.

"What's the conductor doing up there?" Tessie asked, watching the man move from passenger to passenger taking down information.

"Dinner orders," Charlie replied. Tessie's eyebrows furrowed together at his answer as if he might be joking.

"Really?" she questioned.

"Yes, really. The conductor takes down orders and then they're sent ahead to the Harvey House. That way the chef knows in advance how many meals to prepare and the staff can be ready to serve the passengers immediately upon their arrival."

"Mr. Banion, good to see you. Will you be dining at the Harvey House this evening?" the conductor inquired, his friendliness making it obvious that he and Charlie had known each other for some period of time.

"I certainly will, and Dr. Wilshire will be joining me," he answered, indicating his traveling companion across the aisle.

"Doctor, huh? Well, good to have you aboard, Dr. Wilshire," he said, with a nod and looked back toward Charlie.

"You folks going to be eating in the dining room or the lunch room?"

"The dining room," Charlie answered for both of them.

"In that case, I need to know if you'd prefer the baked veal pie, pork with applesauce, or the roast sirloin of beef au jus," he inquired, his pencil poised to take their order.

"Tessie? What sounds good to you?" Charlie inquired.

"I believe I'll have the baked veal pie," she responded.

"Make mine the same," Charlie told the conductor.

"That's two baked veal pies," the conductor repeated. "That comes with asparagus in cream sauce, lobster salad, and your choice of dessert," he proudly announced. "Coffee, tea, or milk?"

Charlie looked over toward Tessie who replied she would like tea and Charlie requested coffee. Having completed their order, the conductor continued down the aisle.

"Look, Addie, see the deer and her baby," Tessie said pointing out the window toward the graceful animals. When no response came from the child she reached over the seat and touched Addie's shoulder to gain the child's attention. Once again she pointed toward the deer and watched Addie smile in delight when she sighted them.

"Pretty, aren't they?" Tessie asked the child.

Addie's face was still pressed against the train window when Lydia came down the aisle and plopped in the seat beside her little sister.

"She won't answer you. She doesn't know you're talking to her—she's deaf," Lydia remarked to Tessie, her voice void of emotion.

"She talked to me earlier," Tessie's replied, sure the statement was untrue.

"Probably read your lips. She wouldn't hear a gunshot if it went off right next to her," Lydia stated coldly.

"I didn't realize, I'm very sorry," Tessie said, saddened by the revelation.

"She gets by all right most of the time. I'm the one that gets stuck with all the worries and she gets all the sympathy," the young woman replied, her resentment toward the child evident. "It's a real pain having to look after her all the time. I'm just hoping I get to keep my job once they find out I brought the brat along. Be just my luck to get fired after doing so well in my training, but maybe they'll have some kind of work for her," she told the captive audience seated behind her.

"I don't know if Fred has anyone that young working for him," Charlie stated, eyeing the girl with a look she interpreted as disapproval.

"Oh, no! Don't tell me you work for Mr. Harvey," Lydia wailed. "I have the worst luck in the world. Who else but me would sit down and pour out their heart to the one person who could ruin everything."

"I don't work for Mr. Harvey," Charlie interrupted. "I work for the Santa Fe railroad but I do know Fred. He's a good man but I don't believe he would want a child Addie's age employed in one of his establishments."

"Whew, that was a close call," Lydia exclaimed. "I can't tell you how relieved I am. You won't tell Mr. Harvey about Addie, will you?"

Charlie met her eyes. "I don't want to see you and your

little sister in dire circumstances, but I'll not lie for you either," he answered.

Lydia glowered at him and began to rise from the seat. "Why don't you sit back down and tell us why you brought Addie with you. It might make it easier for us to help you," Tessie cajoled, hoping to placate the older girl.

Quickly realizing it would be more advantageous to have these folks as friends, Lydia reclaimed her seat and, gazing at some unknown object just behind Tessie's shoulder, launched into her account.

"My parents got divorced about three years ago," she began. "Ma got word about a year later that Pa died. Not that it mattered too much. He never sent any money to help out when he was alive. Mama went to work as a housekeeper and cook for some rich folks in town. They didn't want us living in their fancy house, so Ma rented a small place outside of town. She had to walk over three miles every morning and evening, no matter what the weather was like. Not once did they so much as offer to give her a ride in their buggy, even when it was pouring rain or the snow was a foot deep. Ma never did complain though," she continued, shaking her head in dismay.

"I know that must have been difficult for all three of you," Tessie responded, her heart going out to the two young women.

Lydia didn't respond, but continued in a hollow voice. "About a year ago Ma got sick with influenza. We couldn't afford a doctor, so she just kept getting worse until finally she died."

"Sounds like your mother tried real hard to take care of things on her own," Charlie commented.

"She did, but she needed help and there was never anyone around to give her a hand. It was all she could do to make enough money to pay the rent and buy food. Even when she was hot with fever, she would drag out of bed and go to work," Lydia stated. "After she died, I knew I had to find some way to take care of myself. I had just finished high school and Ma was so proud. She always wanted me to have a better life, but I was left trying to find a place to live and a job that would pay decent wages. A friend told me about an advertisement she had seen for the Harvey Houses. She said it paid good money and you got a place to live. It didn't take me long to make my decision. Course Addie has been my biggest problem, as usual," she said, giving the child a look of disdain.

"I'm sure Addie's had her share of difficulty dealing with your mother's death," Tessie stated, disquieted by older girl's attitude.

"Oh sure, poor little deaf Addie. Let's all feel sorry for Addie," Lydia spat mockingly, while twisting the ties of her bonnet.

Tessie glanced over and saw the look of sadness on Addie's face. The child had been watching her sister's performance and appeared to have a clear understanding of Lydia's truculent attitude.

"I didn't mean to discount the problems you've had to deal with Lydia," Tessie responded soothingly. "I doubt there are few young women your age who could have handled themselves as admirably under the circumstances. Tell me, where did Addie stay while you took your training as a Harvey Girl?" Tessie inquired, hoping to gain further information about their situation.

"She lived with some folks from the church. They said they could keep her while I took my training but they've got ten kids of their own. There's no way they could afford another one. I probably could have found someplace for her if she could hear, but nobody wants an extra kid around if they have problems," Lydia expounded.

"Was Addie born deaf?" Tessie questioned.

"No, she could hear up until a year ago. I don't know what happened. She just couldn't hear anymore," Lydia answered.

"Did she slowly lose her ability to hear? Was she sick and run a high temperature? Did she fall down and hit her head?" Tessie questioned in rapid succession.

"I don't know," Lydia responded, irritated that all of Tessie's interest seemed directed at her sister. "What do you care anyway? It doesn't make any difference when she quit hearing. She can't hear now and she's a pain in the neck!"

"I'm sorry, I certainly didn't mean to upset you," Tessie quickly apologized.

"This woman is a doctor, Lydia. I'm sure that's why she's showing such interest in your sister's ailment," Charlie offered in an attempt to smooth the discussion between the two women.

"A doctor? I don't believe it. A woman doctor, if that don't beat all. Wish you'd have been around when my Ma was so sick," the young woman replied, shaking her head in disbelief. "Where you headed?" she asked Tessie.

"She's going to Florence, same as you," Charlie answered. "Dr. Wilshire's going to be the new physician for the Santa Fe employees," Charlie proudly announced to the young woman.

Tessie sat staring at him, wondering why he felt compelled to answer on her behalf.

"You been a doctor very long?" Lydia inquired.

"No," Tessie and Charlie replied in unison.

"I believe Mr. Banion feels qualified to speak on my behalf since he hastily read my resume a few hours ago," Tessie continued, a grin on her face.

"I'm sorry, that was very rude of me, wasn't it?"

"That's all right. It's just that I've been used to answering for myself the last several years," Tessie remarked, causing all three of them to laugh and relieve some of the previous tension.

"Your folks must have lots of money if they could send you for schooling to be a doctor," Lydia stated, the sound of envy obvious in her voice.

"My parents died when I was twelve years old, Lydia," Tessie answered. "I was very fortunate, however. My Uncle Jon lived on the adjoining farm and our grandmother lived with us also. Then a couple years after my parents died, Uncle Jon married a wonderful woman. Nobody could have asked for a better substitute mother than Aunt Phiney. She encouraged me to use all of my God given talents."

"Yeah, well, my mother didn't have a good job or good luck so now I'm stuck taking care of Addie. But it's my turn now, and I'm not going to let her get in my way. I'm going to work at the Harvey House and meet me a man to take care of me," Lydia retorted, flinging her head in a decisive nod.

Tessie thought the young woman looked almost triumphant—as though she had discovered the secret to a guaranteed happy life. It was obvious Lydia thought the solution to her unhappiness was a husband to take over the burdens and responsibilities that had been thrust upon her. For now, however, she was mistakenly directing her resentment at what she considered the source of her problems—Addie.

"I hope everything will work out for both you and Addie," Tessie stated. "If there is anything I can do to help, I hope you won't hesitate to let me know," Tessie offered. She didn't know what she could do, but certainly both of these sisters needed a friend.

"Thanks," Lydia answered. "Maybe you or your gentleman friend can help me find a way to keep Addie at the Harvey House," she ventured.

"Do you think you could help, Charlie?" Tessie asked, with a look of hopefulness.

"I'll see what I can do," Charlie answered, not certain he could be of much assistance, but wanting to please Tessie. He watched her small smile develop more broadly and her cheeks take on a slight blush, her happiness evident at his remark. "I'm not promising anything," he quickly continued, the remark directed more at Tessie than the two sisters.

"I understand," Tessie interrupted. "I appreciate the fact that you are willing to at least make an attempt."

"Well, don't expect a miracle," he responded.

"Why not? I'm sure God is quite capable of a miracle for these two girls and that may be the very reason you're on this train," Tessie answered in an authoritative manner.

"That may be so," Charlie remarked, "but I had rather hoped it was because we were destined to meet and fall in love," he said, quickly moving across the aisle and firmly squeezing her into the corner of the seat.

"Mr. Banion, just because you have agreed to assist these women does not mean I am giving you permission to make advances toward me," Tessie retorted, attempting to put this brash man in his place.

"Now, Tessie, remember you agreed to call me Charlie," he replied, the humor in his voice causing Lydia to giggle.

"Looks like you've already got you a man," Lydia teased. "I'll go back up with the other women so you two lovebirds can be alone," she said, giving them an exaggerated wink before she turned to move forward with her friends.

"Now look what ideas you've put in her head," Tessie reprimanded, giving a sharp jab with her elbow that landed in Charlie's right side.

"Ouch. I thought you took an oath to heal, not do bodily harm to people," Charlie complained, rubbing the spot where she had inflicted the blow.

"Oh, don't be such a big baby," she chided. "If that's all it takes to turn you into a whimpering soul, you'd better never come to my office for treatment."

He watched her give Addie a quick smile when she noticed the little girl observing their sparring match.

The train whistle exploded in two long blasts, signaling they would soon be arriving at their destination. Tessie watched Addie as another shrill whistle sounded out into the late afternoon dusk, but there was no indication the child heard a sound.

three

Amid clouds of billowing gray smoke, the train came to a hissing, belching stop, allowing the passengers to disembark onto a wooden platform. The sturdy brick station stoically guarded the rails while passengers entered and exited the trains in a flurry of activity.

"Harvey House is just this way," Charlie stated, taking her arm as she stepped down from the train.

The establishment still carried the name Clifton Hotel although Charlie was quick to tell her it bore little resemblance to the old hostelry. Most folks now referred to it as the Harvey House.

The waitresses were dressed just as those Tessie had seen in Topeka. The black and white uniforms, with Elsie collars, black stockings, black shoes, and white ribbons tying back their hair, did little to punctuate the femininity of the young women. The waitresses seemed to weave in and out among the tables with an ease and familiarity which belied the fact most of them had been working for Fred Harvey only a short time. It was a superb testimonial for their training.

Charlie and Tessie were seated at a small table by themselves although most of the passengers were at larger tables, visiting and enjoying the attention being lavished upon them the minute they entered the establishment.

"What do you think of your new community so far?" Charlie asked, pleased that his companion appeared impressed by the surroundings.

"I must say, I am surprised," she exclaimed, delightedly.

"My expectations didn't include dining in such elegance. Who would have expected to find English china and Irish linen on the tables of a restaurant in Florence, Kansas?"

"Not many folks, I suppose," Charlie agreed, "but more and more people will come to expect elegance at all of the stops along the Santa Fe."

Tessie was sure he was right, especially if they all measured up to the bill of fare presented at the Clifton Hotel. "Would you like another cup of tea?" Charlie inquired, hoping she would be willing to linger a few minutes longer.

"If you don't mind, I'd rather get myself settled. It's been a long day and I don't think I could hold another ounce of food or drink," she replied, with a smile.

"I guess I'm just trying to keep you with me as long as possible," Charlie admitted. "I'm sure you're tired and would like to see your new home. Let me introduce you to the chef before we leave," he said, directing her toward the kitchen doorway.

As they approached, Tessie could hear the sound of Lydia's voice coming from the kitchen. It was evident an argument had ensued and, from the sound of things, Lydia had met her match. Just as Charlie opened the kitchen door, Tessie heard someone yelling at Lydia to get her brat out of the kitchen.

"What's the problem, John?" Charlie asked, walking into the kitchen with an air of authority.

"I'm not real sure. From the sound of things, one of the new waitresses has a little sister with her. Guess she thinks Mrs. Winter should allow the kid to stay in the dormitory," replied the chef. "You know that's not gonna happen. Mrs. Winter won't let anyone sleep in those rooms unless they work here. Me?—I'm just trying to stay clear of the ruckus," he stated, shrugging his shoulders and shaking his head in disgust.

"Say, John, would you consider hiring the little girl as a pearl diver?" Charlie asked, hoping the chef's agreement would cancel out Mrs. Winter's objection to Addie living with her sister.

"I don't know. That little tyke couldn't even reach the sinks," he replied.

"What's a pearl diver?" Tessie inquired, wondering if Charlie had lost his senses.

"Oh, that's just a nickname we give the dishwashers," the chef replied, his wide grin revealing a set of uneven white teeth sitting under an inky black moustache.

"Come on, Johnny, she could do it. The kid's probably worked harder in the last year than most of the guys we've got laying track," Charlie exaggerated, hoping to make good on his promise to Tessie and Lydia.

"I suppose we could turn one of those big tubs upside down and let her stand on it," he replied.

It would be good just once to get the upper hand with old Mrs. Winter, decided John. She didn't seem to have much of a heart and John knew she liked the power of her position. If the little girl had a job and was related to one of the Harvey Girls, she would have to let her stay in the hotel with the rest of the hired help, he reasoned to himself. Maybe it would bring her down a peg or two if she realized the employees were going to stick together. Besides, he could use another dishwasher.

"Thanks, John. I owe you one," Charlie responded, giving the chef a slap on the back and extending his hand.

"That's okay, Charlie. She's a cute little kid and we can find something to keep her busy."

The men had just finished their conversation when Mrs. Winter came bustling through the kitchen, obviously a woman intent on getting things settled.

"Ah, Mrs. Winter, you appear to be a bit frazzled this

evening," Charlie crooned. "I would think you'd be in good spirits with all this new help arriving," he added.

"I'm glad to have the additional help, Mr. Banion, but not the additional problems! You can't imagine the difficulties some of these women can create," she stated, grabbing a dish cloth and vehemently rubbing a non-existent spot on one of the counters.

"Perhaps I could be of assistance," Charlie offered, hoping to entice her into conversation regarding young Addie.

"I doubt that—not that you're not capable, mind you. It's just one of these new women brought a young sister with her expecting I'd allow her to live with the rest of us. There are rules, Mr. Banion. Some of these women, especially the new ones, just do not understand rules," she stated, sure she had found a comrade in the personnel manager for the railroad.

"Yes, rules need to be followed. I agree," he stated. "Isn't it a rule that if you work in a Harvey House you live there?"

"Of course," she replied smugly, not realizing she had been caught in his snare.

"Well, then, you have no problem. That little girl is an employee of the House," he retorted, watching as deep lines formed across her forehead.

"How can that be?" she asked, sure there had to be a misunderstanding.

"I hired her. She's gonna be a pearl diver," John answered.

"Whaaat? I don't believe it. She's too little to wash dishes and you know it Johnny," she retorted, angry at the turn of events. The entire staff was now gathered in the kitchen listening to Mrs. Winter receive her come-uppance from the chef. They all knew Johnny was the one person she wouldn't upset. After all, he was one of the country's finest chefs and Mr. Harvey had brought him all the way from Chicago. Mrs. Winter didn't dare cause a problem that would make Johnny unhappy. She turned on her heel and caught Lydia's wide-eyed stare.

"She'll have to sleep in the same bed with you," she directed, her teeth clenched and jaw set.

"I bet you could find a cot somewhere if you tried real hard. After all, we run a hotel," John called after the retreating matron.

"I'll see what I can do," she retorted and marched from the room, trying to maintain an iota of dignity as her staff smiled at the back of the rigid form departing the room.

"I think I may have made an enemy," John stated to no one in particular.

"She'll get over it. Think she needs a few lessons in how to deal with employees," Charlie stated.

Lydia was irritated that Addie had once again caused her trouble, but realized she owed a thank-you to Mr. Banion and the chef. Not wanting to make a spectacle of herself in front of the other employees, she waited until most of them had left the room and then made her way to where John, Charlie, and Tessie were talking. As she approached the trio she noticed Addie standing close by, Tessie's hand resting protectively on the child's shoulder.

"I want to thank you both," Lydia stated, extending her hand first to Charlie and then to John. "It's very kind of you to give my sister a job," she said to the chef.

Pulling Addie beside her and looking directly into her eyes, she stated, "You'll do a good job, won't you, Addie?"

The child nodded in agreement and immediately tried to navigate back to her previous position beside Tessie. Lydia firmly gripped her arm, causing the child to grimace, but she made no sound. Tessie felt anger begin to well up inside but knew it would serve no purpose to confront Lydia. It would only make matters worse for Addie, and she certainly didn't want that to occur.

"I guess it's about time I get you over to your new home," Charlie stated. "It's been a long day and I'm sure you're tired."

"I'm sure we all are. Nice to meet you, John. Good night, Lydia—Addie," Tessie said, her smile directed at the child.

The little girl looked totally bewildered by the events that had taken place in her midst. *I wonder just how much she understood of all that occurred,* Tessie thought as they left the restaurant and walked down the brick sidewalk.

"Your house is nearby. Makes it convenient for you to be close to the station although it's a little noisy when the trains are coming through," Charlie commented.

"I'm sure I'll get used to it. I may have to bury my head under a pillow for the first few nights," she joked.

The night air was warm and they sauntered down the street until Charlie stopped in front of a white frame house with a picket fence and large porch. There were rosebushes on either side of the gate and the honeysuckle was in full bloom, it's sweet fragrance wafting in the breeze.

"This is it!" Charlie announced, pushing open the gate for his companion.

He watched closely for her reaction, not sure why it was so important to him that she like the dwelling. Her shoulders held erect, he couldn't detect a single wrinkle in her navy traveling suit as she walked toward the house. Tiny wisps of coppery hair escaped the blue wool hat she had carefully secured when they disembarked the train. He continued his observation as she peeked around the side of the house and turned to him with a look of delighted expectation.

"It's wonderful, Charlie. If it's only half as splendid inside, I'm going to be extremely pleased," she stated, walking up the front steps, her hips swaying slightly beneath the wool skirt.

"Let me unlock the door for you," he offered, withdrawing a silver skeleton key from his pocket. With a click, the door unlatched and bowing in a grand sweep, Charlie stepped aside, allowing her entrance.

"It's completely furnished, but if you want to bring your own things, we can remove any of the furniture," he said in a rush, not sure she would be pleased with the decor.

Charlie bent down and ignited the lamp just inside the front door. The illumination from the frosted globe mingled with the etched mirror hanging in the hallway, giving the room a scintillating luminescence. Everything from the overstuffed floral divan to the cream colored arm chairs were to her taste. The large oak mirror hanging over the fireplace was flanked on either side by wood framed paintings of the countryside. The kitchen was large enough for a small table and two chairs. There were more shelves than she would ever be able to fill and the pump over the kitchen sink gave her an unimaginable thrill. A home where she wouldn't have to fetch water from the well. *What more could anyone wish for,* she thought, until Charlie escorted her into the fully equipped treatment room and office! It was grand beyond her expectations. There were doctors who had been in practice for years and not enjoyed an office the likes of this.

"Well, what do you think? Sorry you signed that contract?" Charlie asked, feeling assured of her answer.

Not even aware he remained in the room, Tessie moved through the office in a calculated manner, touching and checking each drawer and cabinet, running her fingers over the instruments while taking a mental inventory. Occasionally she would stop and examine some particular item more closely and then continue. Reaching the bookcase, she opened the oak and glass door and removed the books one by one, almost caressing them as she turned the pages.

"It would appear that someone knows how to equip a doctor's office," Tessie commented when she had concluded surveying the rooms.

"I was beginning to think you had forgotten I exist," Charlie replied. "I take it you're willing to remain an employee of the Santa Fe and you're not going to beg me to tear up your contract?" he teased.

"I think I just may be able to force myself to practice medicine here," she answered with a grin that made her appear much younger than her twenty-eight years.

"If you think you know your way around the place well enough, I better get back to the train station. I've got some paperwork to take care of before going back to the hotel," he told her, not wanting to leave but realizing she was weary.

"I'll be just fine. I plan to make an early night of it," she said walking with him toward the front door.

"Please say you'll have breakfast with me," he requested as they reached the porch, not wanting to distance himself from her until he was sure when he would see her again.

"Since I've nothing here to eat, how could I turn down such an invitation," she answered, regretting immediately how coquettish she sounded.

Taking her hand, he lifted it to his lips and gently placed a kiss on her palm. "Until morning," he said, smiling.

Tessie watched after him as Charlie walked down the sidewalk toward the train station and then she sat down on the porch step. The air was warm and she leaned back, looking up at the darkening sky, a few twinkling stars beginning their nightly vigil.

"Thank You, Lord. I don't know what plans You have for me in this place, but thank You for sending me here," she whispered.

four

The morning dawned clear and crisp, a beautiful spring day. Tessie walked out the front door just as Charlie was approaching her new home.

"Beautiful day, wouldn't you say?" Charlie called out as he climbed out of his small horse-drawn buggy.

"Oh, indeed it is! I was going to sit on the porch and enjoy listening to the birds sing until you arrived," she responded.

"Well, I may allow you to do just that," he replied with a grin. "I thought it would be a splendid morning to eat out-doors. I hope you won't think me too forward, but I stopped at the Harvey House and had them pack breakfast for two," he said, producing a wicker basket covered by a large linen napkin.

"What a wonderful idea," she proclaimed, thrilled at his innovative proposal. "Shall we eat here on the porch?" she inquired.

"I think that's an excellent choice, Dr. Wilshire," he responded with mock formality, causing her to giggle.

Tessie moved a plant from the small table sitting on the porch and covered it with a blue and white checked table-cloth she found in the kitchen. From the contents of the bas-ket, it appeared the Harvey House took as much care in preparing breakfast as it did the evening bill of fare. The croissants were light as a feather and the apricot preserves divine. Tessie was amazed at the cup of fresh fruit, knowing most of what she was eating would not be ready for harvest in Kansas for months. She savored every bite and Charlie was pleased he had been the one responsible for providing her such enjoyment.

"That was a delightful surprise, Charlie. Thank you for your thoughtfulness," she said, wiping the corners of her mouth with one of the cloth napkins.

"It was my pleasure. I wish I could extend an invitation for tomorrow morning, but unfortunately, I must get back to Topeka for a few days," he told her.

Tessie was surprised at the sense of disappointment she felt upon hearing those words. "Will you be back soon?" she asked, and then chided herself for being so forward.

"Probably a week to ten days," he answered, "but it's good to know I'll be missed."

"It's just that I assumed you would be here to introduce me to some of the employees, but you needn't give it another thought. I've been on my own in much more foreign environments than Florence, Kansas, and I'm sure things will go splendidly," she responded hastily, not wanting to appear overly interested in Charlie's companionship.

"I don't think you'll need much introduction. The railroaders and their families have been anticipating the arrival of a doctor for several months now. I doubt there's much of anybody in town who doesn't know you moved in last evening. Course, I'm still hoping you're going to miss me just a little," he said, a crooked grin on his face.

"I'm not sure I'd classify myself as moved in just yet. I think I'll need a few more of my belongings before I feel settled," she responded, avoiding his last remark.

"I can understand that," he answered, beginning to place the dishes into the basket. "I'm afraid I must get back to the station. There are a few things I need to complete before the train arrives, but I hope you'll agree to see me when I'm back in town," he said, looking up from the table and meeting her eyes.

"Well, of course, I'll see you. You're a Santa Fe employee," she answered, wanting to avoid a personal commitment. Charlie was a nice man, but things seemed to being moving a little too fast. She had a lot of adjustments to make and Charlie might cloud her judgment. *I'll just have to keep him at arm's length,* she decided.

Charlie smiled and merely nodded at her answer. "I'll see you when I get back to town, Tessie. Don't you let any of those single ruffians from town come calling on you while I'm gone," he added, as he pulled himself up into the buggy and waved to her.

He seems mighty pleased with himself, Tessie thought as she watched the buggy turn and head toward the train station.

❧

Ten days later a strange voice and loud banging on the front door brought Tessie running from the office where she had been making notations in a patient's medical folder.

"Morning, Doc. Hope we ain't disturbing you, but Mr. Banion gave strict instructions that we were to get these trunks over to you as soon as we got the freight unloaded," Howard Malone, one of the new employees, explained.

"You're not disturbing me, Mr. Malone, you are making me immeasurably happy," she answered, delighted to finally have more than two changes of clothing.

"Where you want 'em?"

"If you'll just put the two larger ones here in the parlor and those two smaller ones in my bedroom, I'd be very appreciative," she responded, pointing toward the bedroom doorway.

"Mr. Banion said he would bring over the rest after bit," Howard called over his shoulder, as he carried the last of the two smaller trunks into her bedroom.

"Rest of it? What else was there?" she questioned when

he had returned to the parlor.

"I don't know, ma'am. He just told us to get these trunks over here and he would bring the rest," he repeated. "You need us to do anything else 'fore we get back to work?"

"No, you've been a great help. Thank you again and please tell Mr. Banion I appreciate his kindness."

"Will do, ma'am," he replied, ambling out the door and back toward the train station.

As soon as the door had closed, Tessie raced toward the bedroom and unlocked both of the smaller trunks. It was like Christmas morning with four wonderful gifts to open.

"This is silly, I know what's in all of these trunks," she reprimanded herself aloud, but that didn't squelch the excitement of finally receiving her belongings. Aunt Phiney and Uncle Jon had carefully packed all of her clothing and personal items in the smaller trunks. The two larger ones had not been unpacked since her return home from Chicago after completing medical school.

"I'm glad they only had to pack these two smaller trunks," she mused, digging deeper into the second one. Slowly she pulled out the beautiful quilt she and Aunt Phiney had sewn and lovingly placed it on her bed. It was like greeting an old friend.

"Now, I feel like I'm home," she murmured.

It was almost noon when she finished unpacking the trunks. Undoubtedly she would need to rearrange some of the items but for the present, she was satisfied. Several times throughout the morning her thoughts wandered to what other items could have arrived on the train. It appeared everything was accounted for, including her medical books and a few of her childhood toys that had always given her a sense of comfort. A knock at the door sounded just as she was carrying a small stuffed doll to the bedroom. Giving no heed to her appearance, she opened the door and was met by Charlie's broad smile and an invitation for lunch.

"I couldn't possibly go anywhere looking like this," she stated, catching a glimpse of herself in the hall mirror. "I'd frighten off the rest of the customers!"

"You look beautiful," he retorted, loving the look of her somewhat disheveled hair.

"Why are you standing there like you're hiding something?" she inquired.

"I've brought the rest of your belongings," he said. "Would you care to come out here and take a look?" he asked, grinning at her.

Walking onto the porch, she peeked behind him and spotted a brand new bicycle with a bright red ribbon attached to the seat. Reading the letter that had been tied to the handlebars, she burst forth in gales of laughter. Tears began to stream down her face and she doubled over, unable to control the fit of laughter.

"I know this must be as much a surprise to you as it was to me, but I didn't think you'd find it quite so humorous," he stated when she had finally begun to regain her composure. Hoping she would enlighten him about the gift, Charlie attempted to hide his disappointment when, without a word, she tucked the letter into her pocket.

"Don't I deserve to know the origin of your gift since I served as the delivery boy?" he inquired.

"Certainly," she replied with a smile. "Why don't you come in and have a cup of tea and I'll explain," she offered.

"What about my lunch invitation?" he asked, still hopeful she would accept.

"I really can't leave, Charlie. I have two appointments later this afternoon and need to finish a few things before then. I am a working woman, you remember," she chided.

"Tell you what. I'll leave now and let you get your work

finished if you'll agree to have dinner and spend the evening with me," he bargained.

"Oh, I don't know if I could give you a whole evening," she teased. Charlie's face took on a mock scowl causing her to laugh again. "Okay, it's a deal," she answered. "Now move along and let me get my work completed."

"You sure drive a hard bargain, Dr. Wilshire," he replied, walking out the front door. "I'll be anxious to hear all about this bicycle tonight. Pick you up at six-thirty," he advised, giving her a jaunty salute.

She had to admit it was good to see Charlie. Since their breakfast the morning after her arrival, she hadn't had the pleasure of his company. Now, ten days later, he seemed a familiar face in this new locale. *Be careful,* she thought to herself, *remember you're not going to let things move too quickly.*

It had been a busy and enjoyable time getting her practice set up, although it hadn't been enjoyable making do with only two changes of clothing. She had spent a good deal of time washing and pressing in the last ten days!

By five o'clock Tessie completed her last appointment, cleaned the office, made her notations to the files, and rushed to her room, anxious to decide which of her newly arrived dresses she would wear this evening. She finally chose the lavender with a striped soft silk bodice and skirt. After a quick search, she located her straw hat, adorned with a deep lilac bow. A knock at the door sounded just as she pulled her white gloves from the drawer.

She smiled at Charlie's look of appreciation. "You look like a breath of spring. Shall we enjoy a stroll or would you prefer riding in the carriage?"

"I'd much prefer the walk after being indoors all day," she answered, slipping her hand through the extended crook of his arm.

"Did you by any chance issue any threats to your employees after my arrival?" she inquired as they proceeded down the sidewalk.

"Of course not, what are you talking about?" he inquired.

"I guess I've been surprised how easily the employees and community have accepted a female doctor. It's one of the things my professors drilled into me during medical school—the fact that people did not approve of women doctors and I would never gain their trust," she explained.

Charlie laughed at her answer. "I don't mean to make light of what you've said. I'm sure there are a lot of folks, especially men, who wouldn't take a shine to female doctors. With the additional employees here, folks have been making due with mid-wives or no medical care at all, unless they can force Doc Rayburn out of retirement long enough to treat someone. There wasn't any need for me to issue threats, your training and ability speak for themselves. I had no doubt folks would be pleased to have you as their physician," he stated.

By the time they arrived, the dinner train and its host of travelers had departed, allowing townspeople a quiet enjoyment of the restaurant. Charlie noted the turned heads and stares of admiration as they walked through the restaurant and were seated, although Tessie seemed oblivious. Reaching their table, she scanned the room, hoping to catch a glimpse of Lydia.

"Anything look particularly inviting?" Charlie asked, trying to draw Tessie's attention back to the table.

"Oh, I'm sorry, I haven't even looked at the menu," she apologized, a small smile tracing her lips. "I was hoping Lydia would be working. What are you going to order?"

"Think I'll have the steak but I understand the Chicken Maciel is one of the favorites around here," he replied.

"In that case, I'll try it," she answered, just as Lydia

appeared at their table.

"Evening, Dr. Wilshire, Mr. Banion. Had time to decide on what you'd like?" she asked.

"Sure have," Charlie answered and gave her their order. She poured coffee for each of them and was off in a flurry, taking orders, pouring drinks, and serving meals, the pace never seeming to lose momentum.

When Lydia returned with their meals, Tessie decided she needed to speak quickly or lose the opportunity. "Lydia, would you and Addie like to come for tea next Wednesday afternoon?"

"Me?" the girl asked, seeming amazed at the invitation. Tessie nodded her head, assuring Lydia she had heard correctly.

"What time? I only have a couple hours off in the afternoon, between two and four," Lydia hesitantly answered.

"That would be fine. I don't schedule office visits on Wednesday afternoons, so whenever it's convenient for you and Addie, just stop by," Tessie proposed.

"Right. We'll do that," she responded. She had only taken a few steps when she quickly returned and whispered, "I don't know where you live."

Before Tessie could answer, Charlie spoke up and gave the young woman detailed instructions. Tessie merely shook her head at his obvious need to speak for her.

"I haven't heard about your bicycle as yet," Charlie mentioned as Lydia hastened off to secure two apple dumplings with caramel sauce for their dessert.

"When I first arrived at medical school I met one of the students who had recently graduated and was returning home. He convinced me to purchase his bicycle, expounding upon what a convenience it had proved for him, cycling from his boarding house to classes. I liked the idea of saving time and the fact there would be no additional care and expense with a bicycle." She stopped to taste a forkful of the warm apple dumpling.

"That is sinfully delicious," she stated, pointing her fork at the dessert.

"It is certainly that," Charlie replied. "But, please, back to the bicycle," he prodded.

"Well, never having ridden a bicycle, I had no idea one needed balance, or that a woman's full skirt would cause additional problems. Feeling proud of my frugality, I paid for the bicycle which he delivered to my boarding house. The next morning after breakfast I tossed my books into the basket and began the ride of my life!"

An enormous knowing smile sprawled across Charlie's face. "That must have been quite a sight," he exclaimed, bursting into laughter, the surrounding dinner guests eyeing him as if he had lost his senses.

"It's obvious you have a good idea just how graceful I appeared," Tessie commented. "I'm not sure what was injured most, my knees or my pride—not to mention the new skirt and stockings I ruined," she continued, now joining him in laughter, tears beginning to collect in the corner of each eye. Intermittently interrupted by spurts of laughter, she confessed that she began wearing bloomers when cycling, although it was frowned upon by her instructors. "I was required to change into a skirt as soon as I arrived at school, but it was decidedly worth that concession since once I learned to stay astraddle the contraption, I did save immeasurable time."

"Why did your aunt and uncle think you would want another bicycle?" he questioned.

"Both of them are open-minded enough to think wearing bloomers is appropriate attire for riding a bicycle and they are frugal enough to realize a bicycle is more economical than feeding and caring for a horse. Besides, they knew I enjoyed bicycling once I conquered the metal beast. I traded mine for a medical book before leaving Chicago and had mentioned on several occasions that I missed the exercise and freedom it afforded me," she replied.

"In that case, I would say they've given you a fine gift," he responded, as they rose to leave the restaurant.

Catching Lydia's eye, Tessie raised her hand and called out, "See you and Addie on Wednesday."

Lydia nodded and smiled as she continued jotting down another customer's order.

"Why the persistence about Lydia coming to visit?" Charlie inquired.

"I'm concerned about Addie and how she's managing with all the changes in her life. Lydia seems to resent being thrust into the role of provider. Perhaps if I can ease the burden a bit for Lydia, it will make things better for both of them," she declared, not wanting to discuss the topic further.

"You need to be careful about over-involvement. I'm sure Lydia is the type to take advantage," he counseled.

"I think I'm quite capable of deciding my level of involvement with people," she responded, irritated with his condescending manner.

"I didn't mean to interfere," he apologized. "It's just my nature, I guess."

Tessie didn't respond but tucked his words away for future reference. *If it's his nature to interfere,* she thought to herself, *I'm not sure he's the man for me.*

"I'll be leaving in the morning, but I'll be back late Wednesday afternoon," Charlie said, bringing her back to the present. "How about dinner?" he asked.

"I suppose that would be fine," she answered without much fervor. She was thinking about the upcoming visit with Addie and Lydia rather than her handsome escort.

"Here we are," Charlie announced as he leaned down and unlatched the gate, hoping for an invitation to sit on the porch and visit a while longer.

"So we are. Thank you for dinner, Charlie. I hope you have a good trip tomorrow. See you next week," she stated, without any hint of wanting to prolong the evening.

"Good night," Charlie called back as she entered the front doorway, hopeful she would forget his transgression by the time he returned.

ॐ

Wednesday afternoon finally arrived and Tessie found herself peeking out the lace curtains in the parlor every five minutes, hoping to glimpse her expected visitors. She had almost decided they wouldn't arrive, when a light knock sounded at the front door.

"I had almost given up," she said, smiling at the two girls as she led them into the parlor.

"We can't stay long 'cause I have to be back in half an hour," Lydia replied. "A friend of mine came through on the train and I wanted to visit with him. That's why we're late," she explained.

"How wonderful! Is it someone from back home?" Tessie asked, excited the girls had a friend that was interested in their welfare.

"No, he's a salesman I met since working at the restaurant. We've gone on a couple outings when he's stayed over a few days. We're going out after work tonight," Lydia answered, obviously pleased with her suitor.

"That's nice, Lydia. Does he sell his goods to Mr. Alexander at the general store?"

"Oh, no. He sells at the Harvey House. There's a room where the salesmen setup their merchandise when they're traveling through and townspeople can stop by and do their shopping. You ought to come over and see all the things they have for sale. There's almost always someone setup there," she stated, all the while her eyes darting about the house, clearly impressed with the furnishings.

Tessie placed a cool glass of lemonade in front of Addie and poured cups of tea for Lydia and herself. A large plate of freshly baked cookies sat in front of them, although neither of the women reached for one until they'd been offered.

"What have you and Addie been doing in your spare time?" Tessie asked, watching the younger girl devour her cookie.

"Gosh, I'm so tired by the time I get off my shift, I just about fall into bed at night," Lydia exclaimed. "I'm off a couple hours in the afternoon and that's it except for my one day off. Even when we don't have customers, we've got to polish silver, set tables, scrub counters, and change linens. Course if Floyd's in town, I squeeze in a little time for fun where I can," she said, flipping her head to one side. "When I get married, I'll have a house as nice as this," she proclaimed.

"I'm sure you will," Tessie responded. "And what about Addie? Is she working all the time also?"

"No. I told 'em she could but John, the chef, said she was too little for long hours. He's got her washing dishes for the first two trains each day, then she's done. I should have it so good!"

"What's she do then?" asked Tessie.

"That's exactly my point. She's not doing anything. She could be making extra money if that silly chef would just let her work the same hours as everyone else. I get off work all worn out and she's been lolling around and thinks I should entertain her. On my day off she thinks she should come along with me, even if I'm with Floyd," Lydia replied, giving the smaller girl an accusatory look.

"Perhaps I could help out, Lydia. You could send Addie over here when she gets through in the morning and on her day off. She could play outdoors and keep more active here. Then perhaps she would be ready for bed when you get off work," Tessie offered.

The young woman looked at her suspiciously, not sure why she would make such a generous offer. "I don't know. She gets Sundays off—wouldn't you know she would get Sundays off? Me—I get Tuesday," she responded, not giving a definite answer. "Why you want her around?" she asked, a hint of jealousy creeping into her voice.

"I'm just trying to think how I could help out, Lydia. You're more than welcome to visit anytime too," she responded, trying to relieve any hostility the offer might have induced.

"Guess it wouldn't hurt to give it a try. She would be out of my way. I'll send her over tomorrow afternoon," she stated.

"Why don't we ask Addie if she would like to spend some of her time here? She may be unwilling," Tessie suggested.

"She does what she's told," Lydia replied emphatically, giving the child a quick glare.

Ignoring Lydia's reply Tessie turned toward Addie, making sure the child could read her lips. "Would you like to come to my house each day after work?"

Addie immediately looked toward her sister for the correct answer. From the corner of her eye Tessie watched Lydia mouth the word "yes" and that was followed by Addie nodding her head up and down.

"We gotta go. I'm going to be late for work if I don't get moving," Lydia pronounced, jumping up from her chair and grabbing Addie's arm.

"I'll send her over tomorrow. Thanks for the tea and

cookies," she stated, all the while walking toward the door with the her sister in tow.

"Thank you both for coming," Tessie responded, watching as the two sisters went running down the sidewalk toward the Harvey House.

Walking into her house, Tessie looked at the large clock sitting on the mantel. She had several hours before Charlie would arrive for their dinner engagement. Plenty of time to get a few chores done and catch up on some reading, she determined, picking up the teacups and plates.

❧

If nothing else he's certainly punctual, Tessie decided when Charlie knocked on the front door at exactly 6:30 P.M. *I shouldn't be angry with him for being on time. It's not his fault that I read too long and now I'm rushing around like a chicken with its head cut off,* she mused.

The second loud knock did nothing toward helping her gain a modicum of composure. She rushed to the door, still struggling with the small pearl buttons on the sleeve of her champagne silk shirtwaist.

"I was beginning to think you'd found a better offer," Charlie greeted, holding out a small bouquet of spring flowers. "I hope I didn't rush you," he continued, noting she appeared somewhat disconcerted.

"What? Oh, no—it's my fault. I lost all sense of time when I began reading an article in the medical journal. Why don't you come in while I get my hat and gloves and we can be on our way," she offered.

"What is it you were reading about?" Charlie inquired as they sauntered toward the restaurant.

Immediately, Tessie's face lit up. "I've found the most interesting commentary about deafness. It's written by a highly respected Chicago physician who has been studying deaf patients for a number of years. He and several of his colleagues collaborated on the article," she related with great enthusiasm.

"I see," Charlie replied, squelching his desire to once again admonish her about becoming overly involved with Lydia and Addie.

Tessie didn't miss his lack of excitement about the subject matter. When Lydia came to their table shortly thereafter and whispered that she would send Addie over after lunch the next day, his jaw visibly tightened.

"What else have you been up to aside from mothering the Baker sisters?" he inquired with more sarcasm than he had intended. As soon the words were spoken, he wanted to retract them.

Tessie stiffened and stared directly into Charlie's gray eyes. "I think there needs to be some clarification about our relationship if we're to continuing seeing each other on a social basis, Mr. Banion," Tessie stated quite formally.

"I'm sorry—" Charlie began.

"No, please don't interrupt me. You need to understand I am open to listening to your opinions. I will then evaluate that information based on my education and beliefs. I am not, however, willing to allow you or any other person to impose ideas and beliefs upon me."

Holding up her hand to ward off his attempt to speak, she continued, "I won't allow you to make me feel foolish or imprudent because I want to befriend two young women. If that makes you uncomfortable, I don't think we should see each other again," she finished.

Charlie leaned back in his chair, now certain the tales he had heard about redheads and their tempers had some validity. "I truly am sorry," he declared. "You are absolutely correct that I have no right to impose my opinions upon you, and perhaps that is what I've been doing. For that I apologize. You, however, have been extremely defensive when I've attempted to discuss Addie and Lydia. I merely wanted to point out that sometimes it is wise to move forward cautiously in order to prevent being hurt or exploited by others."

"Does that apply to you as well as Lydia and Addie?" she inquired.

"Well, no, of course not. I. . .I," he stammered and then looked up when he heard her giggle.

"You see, Charlie," she said, "I don't know any more about you than I do of Lydia and Addie. If you're willing to trust my judgment of people in befriending you, I hope you will extend that trust to my companionship with Lydia and Addie."

"I guess you've got me," he answered with a grin. "Tell you what, I'll try to keep my mind open if you'll promise to keep your eyes open. How about it?"

"I think that will work," she replied.

I truly hope so, Charlie thought to himself, sure that Lydia Baker was interested in more than Tessie's friendship.

five

Shortly after lunch the next day, Addie appeared at Tessie's front door in a tattered, brown print dress, her hair damp from leaning over steamy dishwater all morning.

"Good afternoon, Addie," Tessie greeted as she swung open the front door.

"Hi," Addie responded hesitantly. "How come you want me to come here?" she bluntly asked before entering the house.

"Because we're both new in town and I know I could use a friend. How about you?" Tessie answered, extending her hand to the child.

"I guess we could try, but I've never had a friend as old as you," the child innocently replied, causing Tessie to laugh. Addie wasn't sure what was so humorous, but she smiled and entered the house.

"Is there something special you'd like to do this afternoon?" Tessie asked, but when Addie didn't answer, she realized she had not been heard. *I must remember to gain her attention before speaking,* Tessie reminded herself and then touched the child's arm.

"What would you like to do today?" she repeated, looking directly into the small brown eyes.

Addie merely shrugged her shoulders in response, leaving the decision to Tessie.

"I have several patients I'll need to see in my office a little later," she told the youngster "but I do have a few playthings from when I was a little girl."

"Do you have a ball?" Addie asked. "I like to play outside

when it's nice, but Lydia always makes me go upstairs and take a nap," she said, beginning to loosen up with her new friend.

"I think I may have one," Tessie answered, pulling a cloth bag out of the hallway closet. "Why don't you look through here and find what you'd like to play with. I have a patient arriving, but if you need me just come through that door to the office," she said, pointing toward the office entrance.

"Okay," Addie responded, obvious her thoughts were on the toys and nothing else.

Tessie checked on Addie several times throughout the day and the two of them enjoyed lemonade on the front porch between appointments. Addie seemed content and Tessie was savoring their brief visits between patients.

"What's that you're doing there?" Charlie called out, forgetting for the moment Addie could not hear him. Tessie looked up from her desk at the sound of his voice and watched as Charlie walked over toward a spot in the yard where Addie was sitting. The child noticed him as he drew closer, and waved her hand in recognition.

"I'll play you a game," Charlie said kneeling down beside her. Having found a small bag of marbles among Tessie's old toys, Addie located a spot alongside the house where there were a few weeds, but the grass had failed to grow. Meticulously she had pulled the weeds, and now sat shooting the round balls, thoroughly enjoying the sunshine and new found entertainment.

"Okay," she told Charlie, and watched as he drew a circle in the dirt.

"Let me show you how this is done," he said, patiently explaining the finer points of how to shoot a good game of marbles.

Tessie sat listening through the open window in her

office. When she had completed writing notes in a file, she walked out to the join them. "Good afternoon, Charlie," she welcomed. "What caused this unexpected visit?" she inquired, pleased to see Addie enjoying the game.

"No frivolous chit-chat while I'm concentrating on my game," he admonished, giving her a winsome grin. Addie fervently watched as he made the shot.

"You lose," she said, clapping her hands together.

"That's because I taught you too well," he said, gathering her into his arms and giving her a spontaneous hug. Tessie stood watching as the small child clung to his neck, hungry for the love and attention she had been denied since her mother's death.

"I assume it's been a good first-day visit," Charlie questioned, Addie still clinging to him.

"It has gone very well. Thank you for being so kind," Tessie responded, looking down at the small figure tightly clutching him.

"I'm going to be leaving for Topeka in an hour, but I'll be back this weekend. I know that Addie will be with you all day on Sunday so I was wondering if I might accompany the two of you to church and then we could go on a picnic," he ventured, hopeful she would think it was a good idea.

"That would be wonderful," she exclaimed. "If, by chance, the weather doesn't cooperate with a picnic, we can eat here," she suggested.

"Great. I'll come by for you at ten o'clock but don't you cook, even if the weather is bad. I'll make arrangements with John over at the Harvey House to fix up a basket lunch and if it rains, we'll have our picnic indoors," he told her. "I better get going or I'll not be ready to leave when the train pulls out," he advised with a smile. "I'll see you both on Sunday," he told her and then leaned down and said, "I'll be by to pick you up for church on Sunday,

Addie," and gave the child a hug.

"I don't want to go to church," the child informed Tessie shortly after Charlie's departure.

"Why not?" Tessie questioned.

"Lydia makes me go by myself and the kids make fun of my clothes and call me a dummy," she replied honestly, the pain evident in her eyes.

"Sometimes people don't realize how much they hurt us with their words," Tessie told the child. "You must always remember that you are special. God made only one Addie Baker and He loves her very much. Even though other people hurt your feelings, you can always depend on God and know He loves you just the way you are," she counseled the child.

"Does He love those kids that were mean to me?" Addie asked.

"Yes, Addie, He loves them too. He doesn't love the sinful things any of us do but He never stops loving us. God will forgive us for doing wrong if we just ask Him, but He does expect us to try and do better the next time," she instructed.

"Well, I don't love them. I don't even like those naughty kids, and I don't want to go to church and be around them," Addie said, a tear sliding down her cheek.

"I know, Addie. It's harder for us to forgive people. God does a much better job, but He would want you to try and forgive the mean actions of those children. He certainly wouldn't want the actions of others to keep you from worshiping Him. Besides, Charlie and I will be with you this time. Will you try it just this once?" Tessie cajoled.

"If you promise I can sit between you and Charlie, so they won't see me," Addie bargained.

"Absolutely," Tessie agreed. "And after church we'll go on a picnic. Would you like that?"

"Oh, yes!" the child exclaimed, jumping up and down.

"Oh, yes, yes."

&

Bright and early Saturday morning, Tessie paid a visit to the general store. She found a Liberty-print cotton dress with contrasting blue silk sash that looked as though it would be a perfect fit for Addie. At the end of the aisle she spotted a straw cartwheel hat with a ribbon the same shade of blue. Without a moment's hesitation, she purchased both items, along with a pair of child-sized black cotton stockings and a white muslin petticoat.

"Is there anything else I can help you find, Dr. Wilshire?" Mr. Alexander, the owner of the general store, offered.

"No, I think that will be all," she responded, pleased with her purchases.

While Mr. Alexander was wrapping the items, Mrs. Alexander stepped behind him, peering over his shoulder.

"I didn't know you had anyone that small living with you, Doctor," the woman remarked, the curiosity notice-able in her voice.

"I don't have any one of any size living with me, Mrs. Alexander," Tessie responded, irritated by the woman's intrusive manner. Mrs. Alexander was known for collecting gossip while working in her husband's store and passing it along to anyone who would lend an ear. Tessie did not intend for her business to become grist for the town rumor-mongers.

Mr. Alexander handed her the purchases and gave his wife a stern look of disapproval. *At least he doesn't con-done her meddling behavior,* Tessie thought as she turned and exited the store.

&

A light knock at the door Sunday morning made Tessie wonder if someone other than Addie had come calling. Although she had only been coming to the house a few days, Tessie had instructed her there was no need to knock.

"Come in, Addie," she offered. Addie stood looking up at her in the same brown dress she had worn for several days, having made a valiant effort to adorn herself by placing a small ribbon around her head.

"You look very nice," Tessie told her. "I hope you won't mind, but I was in the general store yesterday and saw a dress I thought might fit you. It was so pretty I couldn't resist," she told the youngster. "Would you like to see if you like it? If it fits, you could wear it to church. That is, if you want to," Tessie continued, leading her into the spare bedroom where the dress, hat, and undergarments lay on the bed.

Nothing could have prepared Addie for the thrill of receiving that beautiful new dress and hat. Once Tessie had tied the blue silk sash and placed the straw hat upon her curly chestnut tresses, she took the child and stood her before the mirror. Leaning down and placing her head behind Addie's shoulder, they looked at their reflections staring back at them.

"You look lovely," Tessie told her.

"Almost as pretty as you?" the child questioned, tipping her head back to look into Tessie's eyes.

"Much prettier," Tessie answered. "Now, come along," she said, extending her hand toward the child's, just as Charlie came bounding up the front steps.

"I have to be the luckiest man in all of Kansas," he exclaimed to the pair. "There's no other man who has the good fortune to escort such beautiful women. Turn around for me, Addie," he instructed, twirling the child in front of him.

"Tessie got me these new clothes," she proudly announced.

"And you look magnificent in them," he responded,

catching Tessie's eye and giving her a smile.

His reaction pleased Tessie, who had expected him to give her a reproachful look or once again caution her about the "Baker sisters."

The day flew by quickly. Tessie had been good to her word and allowed Addie to sit between the two adults. Although it wasn't Charlie's choice of seating arrangement, he did, however, bow to Tessie's wishes once again. While at the park, he was attentive to Tessie, but included Addie in the conversation and even took her down to a small stream to wade for a short time. Although he didn't know it, his tolerance and thoughtfulness did not go unnoticed. Tessie knew she was beginning to care more deeply about him than she had anyone for many years.

"I think perhaps we should be heading home," she told the pair as they returned from the stream. "I packed up the picnic basket while you too were off exploring. It's almost time for you to catch your train, isn't it?" she asked Charlie.

"I'm afraid so. I'll be glad when I can quit traveling quite so much," he acknowledged as they walked toward the carriage.

"That will be nice," she answered, squeezing his arm and giving him an inviting smile.

Addie had been particularly careful not to soil her new dress and as soon as they arrived at the house, she announced she was going to change into her old dress and went running off to the bedroom.

"I had a wonderful time today, Tessie, and I hope there will be many more in store for us," Charlie said, cupping her face in his large hands and placing a tender kiss on her lips. "You're very special," he told her, gathering her into his arms.

Tessie felt as though she could stay wrapped in his protection forever and, although she enjoyed the sensation, it confused her. She had always been so independent, never allowing herself to become overly-involved with a man and now, here she was not wanting Charlie to leave. It made no sense. *I hardly know him,* she thought to herself as Addie came bounding out of the bedroom.

"I'd like a hug, too," she told the pair.

"Well, of course," Charlie answered with a smile, opening his arms as she came running across the room toward him.

"Would you like something to eat?" Tessie inquired shortly after Charlie left.

"I'm not hungry," Addie responded, walking through the room, running her hand across different pieces of furniture and wandering into Tessie's bedroom. She stared at the quilt that covered the four-poster bed and traced her fingers over the intricate design.

"This is very pretty," she told Tessie. "I've never seen anything this pretty on anyone's bed."

Turning to face Addie, Tessie said, "My mother and my Aunt Phiney and I all worked on this quilt and it is very special because lots and lots of love went into it. If you like to sew, perhaps you and I could make a quilt. What do you think about that idea?" she asked the child.

"I only know how to sew a little. Mama didn't have much time to show me but I learn quick," Addie responded expectantly.

"I didn't know a lot about sewing when I started on this quilt either," she told Addie. "I think you'll do a wonderful job. Tell you what, I'll find some fabric and we'll get started next week. Would that be all right?"

"Oh, yes," Addie answered, clapping her hands in delight. "I promise I'll work hard on it."

"I'm sure you will," Tessie answered, just as a knock sounded at the front door.

"There's someone at the door, I'll be right back," she told the child and quickly walked to the parlor and opened the door.

"Evening, Dr. Wilshire," Lydia said, "hope you weren't real busy. This is Floyd, I told you about him. . .the salesman I met at the Harvey House. We're going to town for a while, so would you mind just taking Addie back over to the hotel when you get tired of her?" Lydia pressed herself close to Floyd and give him a sensual smile. Tessie noticed the young man seemed embarrassed by Lydia's advances, but his embarrassment didn't deter her seductive behavior.

"I'll be happy to walk her back, but I thought you had to work this evening," Tessie inquired after hearing Lydia's plans.

"I traded with Lucy," she answered. "Floyd has to leave at ten o'clock and Lucy owed me a favor."

"You two have a nice time," Tessie replied and watched as they walked down the steps, Lydia clearly attempting to captivate the young man.

Addie was peeking around the doorway, pleased that Lydia hadn't come to escort her back to the hotel. "Where's my sister going?" the youngster inquired.

"She and Floyd are going into town for a while so I'll walk you back to the hotel a little later. Will that be all right with you?"

Addie nodded her head up and down and sat down in the parlor, facing Tessie. "Tell me about making your quilt," she requested.

"Well, let's see. I'm not sure how to begin," Tessie remarked.

"At the beginning," Addie responded laughingly.

"You're right; I'll do just that," Tessie replied. "When I was a little older than you my mother began making the quilt that's on my bed, but she died before it was completed."

"Just like my mama?" Addie asked, the tearful sound of her voice making Tessie's heart ache.

"Yes, Addie, just like your mama."

"Did your papa run off and leave you, too?" the child inquired.

"No, I had a wonderful papa, but he died at the same time as my mother. They were in an accident," she answered.

"Oh, that was hard for you wasn't it?" Addie asked, her perception surprising Tessie.

"Yes, it was very difficult. There were five of us children and I was the oldest. My grandmother lived with us and my Uncle Jon had a small house on the land adjoining ours. He and Granny were left to raise all five of us and Granny's health wasn't good. So, Uncle Jon decided to advertise in the newspaper looking for a young woman to come and help Granny with the chores and all of us children."

Addie sat in front of her, eyes held wide open, not wanting to miss anything that Tessie related. "Then what happened?" she asked anxiously.

"Uncle Jon finally got a letter about a young woman who he and Granny thought would be suitable. So, he left and went to Illinois to fetch her. Well, I didn't want any other woman coming into our house trying to take the place of my mother so when Uncle Jon returned, I was very hateful to the young woman. No matter what she did, I wouldn't let her become my friend, but she did have a beautiful quilt on her bed that I truly admired," Tessie related.

"Was it as pretty as yours?" the child inquired, sure that would be impossible.

"I don't think so," Tessie answered. "But, I'm sure Aunt

Phiney thinks her quilt is prettiest, because it's special to her. One day I told Granny I thought Aunt Phiney's quilt was beautiful. After I'd told her that, my grandmother showed me the quilt my mother had begun and suggested that Aunt Phiney and I complete it for my bed. Well, I wouldn't hear of it. I said I didn't want Aunt Phiney touching anything that had belonged to my mother."

"That wasn't very nice, was it?" Addie inquired shaking her head negatively.

"No. But it wasn't until Aunt Phiney showed me she was willing to die in my place, that I finally believed she truly cared for me. It was after that the two of us set to work on the quilt. Aunt Phiney said it was sewn with threads of love because the two of us really learned to love each other while making that quilt. It took us a while but we finally finished, and it's been my constant companion ever since," Tessie concluded.

"I'd like to have something like that to keep with me always," Addie quietly commented.

"You will. It may take some time, but you will. I promise," Tessie answered. "I better get you back to the hotel or you're going to miss curfew, young woman!"

❧

In the weeks that followed Addie proved herself a quick study and Tessie was constantly amazed at the child's proficiency with a needle and thread. She would sit quietly watching Tessie and then take up her needle and thread with the expertise of an age-old quilter. Although most of the quilts Tessie had worked on were made from scraps, she had carefully chosen the colors and fabrics for Addie's, wanting it to be very special. She had finally settled on cotton prints of lavender, pale blue, and shades of pink. Tessie convinced herself they could conquer the double wedding ring pattern, and so far she was right.

"Are you going to make me hear again?" Addie asked one crisp fall afternoon as the two of them sat in Tessie's parlor.

The question startled Tessie for although she had extensively examined Addie on several occasions, the child had never hinted at such an expectation.

"I don't know if I can do that," she responded, wishing she could give the answer Addie longed for.

"You make everyone else well," came Addie's quick rebuttal.

"Not quite everyone. There are some things I can't heal, but I promise you, Addie, I will do all I can," Tessie concluded, hoping God would provide the answer her medical journals had failed to give her.

six

"Doc, come quick! Levi Wilson is mighty sick and he needs a doctor now!" shouted Joe Carlin, the local blacksmith, as he came racing toward the house in a buggy drawn by a sleek black horse. The smithy pulled the animal to a rapid halt in front of the house where it immediately began snorting and pawing at the dirt, anxious to again run at full speed.

"Let me get my bag. Addie, get in the buggy," she mouthed to the child who had arrived only minutes earlier. Rushing into the house Tessie grabbed her bag and some additional medical supplies. Running toward the carriage, she lost no time issuing orders to the blacksmith.

"What do you know about his problem?" she asked as the buggy sped out of town.

"Can't breath. I hear tell he's had breathing problems for quite a spell now," the blacksmith advised.

Tessie merely nodded, not sure what to expect but hoping her skills would serve her well. Once the carriage was drawn to a halt in front of a wooden shanty that appeared to be no bigger than one room, she didn't have long to contemplate her abilities. Jumping down, all three of them made their way inside and found the patient sitting up battling for breath. A hasty examination revealed a goiter which was almost concealed in the chest cavity. The room certainly was not appropriate for an operating room, but Tessie knew that if something wasn't done quickly her patient would die. Issuing a hasty prayer for direction, she turned to the blacksmith and ordered him to remove the door from its hinges and motioned Addie to carry out several wooden boxes. Tessie placed water on the store to boil and found two barrels which she then moved outdoors.

"Place the door across these two barrels," she instructed, as she pulled a sheet from the items she had gathered from home. With a snap of her wrists she watched it flutter across the makeshift operating table. Placing her instruments on the boxes Addie had carried outdoors she watched as the smithy helped Mr. Wilson onto the hastily constructed table.

"Mr. Wilson, I'll be back shortly. I need to scrub my hands before proceeding. Addie, come along, you'll need to scrub also. Stay with him," she instructed the black-smith, walking toward the dilapidated house.

"Addie, stand by the instruments, I'll need your help. You, too," she instructed the blacksmith who was heading back toward the house, not sure he wanted to be a part of the unfolding events.

After administering ether, Tessie made an incision exposing the goiter which was resting on his windpipe. The mass appeared to be about the size of an apple and with only small artery forceps, she realized it would be impossible to grasp and remove it. She stood staring at the object, unsure how to proceed.

Lord, I don't know what to do. Show me how to help this man, she silently prayed.

No more had her prayer been issued than a tiny feather floated down directly under Mr. Wilson's nose. The incision Tessie made permitted her patient to breath in enough air so that when the feather tickled his nose, Levi Wilson burst forth with a stupendous sneeze. As his large chest contracted, the goiter shot so far out that it lay fully exposed in the wound. Tessie quickly seized it with one hand, grabbed her instruments to clamp the lower vessels with her other hand, and completed the remainder of the surgery uneventfully.

"I believe we've had a successful surgery," she announced to the blacksmith, who had turned ashen. "There's no reason you need to remain close by, if you'd like to check on your horse, Mr. Carlin," which was all the encouragement the smithy needed to get away from the makeshift operating room.

"I'll help you clean up, if you tell me what to do," Addie offered, never wavering from her duty station.

"Thank you, Addie. You can wrap those instruments and put them back in my bag. We'll clean and sterilize them at home," she instructed, finishing the sutures on Mr. Wilson's incision.

"Anything I need to be doing?" the blacksmith called out from in front of the shanty.

"Why don't you see if you can find a neighbor who can come over? He should have someone stay with him, unless you'd like the job," Tessie answered.

"Think I better try and locate a neighbor. I'm not too good with sick folks," he responded.

"Really? I hadn't noticed," Tessie answered, giving him a quick grin.

Mr. Wilson had regained consciousness when his neighbors, the Madisons, arrived with the blacksmith. Mr. Madison and Joe supported and half-carried the patient into the house and placed him on the bed which Mrs. Madison had quickly covered with clean linens. Tessie gave her a grateful smile.

"If you two men will dismantle my outdoor operating room, I'll go over the patient care instructions with Mrs. Madison," she directed.

It was obvious Mrs. Madison had taken care of more than a few medical emergencies and Tessie knew Mr. Wilson would be in good hands.

"I don't think I'll need to see you again, Mr. Wilson. Mrs. Madison has assured me she's removed many stitches and she lives much closer than I, so I'll leave you to her care."

He nodded his head, and whispered his thanks for her good care.

"I think you owe your thanks to the Lord," Tessie advised. "He's the one who deserves credit for the success. Some-day when you're in town, I'll explain," she told him, as he drifted back to sleep.

It was supper time when the trio finally loaded back into the buggy and headed for town.

"That was quite a spectacle," the smithy said admiringly.

"Well thank you, Mr. Carlin. I appreciate your assistance," Tessie replied, realizing the blacksmith was genuinely surprised at her ability.

"Thank you too, Addie," she said placing her arm around the child and hugging her close. Addie merely nodded, but her eyes were full of adoration

The buggy pulled to a stop in front of the house and the blacksmith quickly jumped down, lifted Addie to the ground, and assisted Tessie. "It's been a real pleasure, ma'am. If I'm ever in need of a doctor, I sure hope you're the one I get," he stated.

"Well, I hope you won't be needing my services, but I sincerely thank you for the compliment," she replied, feeling embarrassed by his continued adulation. "Come along, Addie, let's make some dinner, you must be starved," she said to the child, taking her hand and walking toward the house.

Addie proved an able assistant in the kitchen and within a short time they had prepared a fine meal. "You are such a fine helper. I don't know what I would have done without you today," she praised the child.

"I like helping you," Addie answered, beginning to clear the table.

"Let's leave the dishes, Addie. I can do them after you go home. Why don't we just sit on the porch and enjoy the evening breeze. There hasn't been much time to visit and enjoy each other today," she said as they walked outdoors.

"Could I be a doctor someday?" Addie asked as they settled on the swing.

Tessie's mind reeled. Without the ability to hear, how could anyone be a doctor, let alone make it through college and medical school? How should she answer without destroying a young girl's dreams? *Help me, Lord,* she silently prayed.

"I believe that with God's help we can do anything. You must remember that sometimes God has very special plans for us and even though we don't understand them, He knows best," she answered.

"I think God wants me to be a doctor and that's why we've become friends," the child answered, obviously pleased with her deduction.

"You could be right," Tessie answered, hoping the child would not be disappointed while, at the same time, she mentally chastised herself for not doing further research into the article on deafness she had read in the medical journal.

❧

"I have an idea for some fun this afternoon," Tessie told her young visitor as they finished a glass of lemonade several days later.

"What?" Addie inquired, her interest peaked.

"Come outside and I'll show you," Tessie responded.

Striding toward the house, Charlie smiled as he watched Addie attempting to gain her balance on Tessie's bicycle. Tessie was running alongside holding onto the handlebars and back of the seat. From the look of things, he wasn't sure if they were having fun or punishing themselves.

"Let me help," he offered, coming upon them and grabbing the handlebars just in time to prevent a collision with a large elm tree.

"That would be wonderful," Tessie admitted, gasping for breath.

When Addie finally arrived at a point where she was able to stay astride the bicycle for a short period of time without teetering to one side or the other, they decided to rest and hoped she wouldn't want another lesson until some time in the future.

"Addie tells me this was your idea," Charlie said, plopping down on a chair in the parlor, still short of breath.

"Yes, I thought it would be something special for her. Obviously, I didn't think it out very well," she admitted sheepishly.

"It will be wonderful for her, but I believe she either needs to be a bit taller or the bicycle a bit smaller. It seems to me her legs aren't quite long enough, but she doesn't want to give up."

"Perhaps I can temporarily delay future rides until she's grown a bit," Tessie responded.

"By the way, I heard quite a story about you two shortly after my arrival this morning," he said, changing the subject.

"What's about?" she inquired, not sure she liked the idea of folks telling stories regarding her or Addie.

"Seems you've garnered quite a reputation for yourself. Joe Carlin, the blacksmith, is telling everyone he meets what a miracle worker you are; how you saved Levi Wilson's life operating on him out in the back yard," he related.

"Well, it's very kind of Joe to give me the credit, but I

told Mr. Wilson and Mr. Carlin that if it hadn't been for God's help, I'd have never successfully completed that operation," she told Charlie.

He listened intently as she related the events surrounding Levi Wilson's ailment and the ensuing surgery. "Sounds to me like you, a bird with a loose feather, and the good Lord worked hand-in-hand on that one," he responded as she finished the tale.

"I was fortunate to have Addie with me, also," she told Charlie. "She became quite an assistant," Tessie praised, giving Addie a smile.

"I must say I am surprised to see you today. I don't recall you mentioning a trip to Florence this week," Tessie stated inquiringly.

"It wasn't planned in advance, but there were some things that needed attention. Besides, it meant an opportunity to visit with you," he said. "I hope you're pleased by the surprise."

"I'm always pleased to see you, Charlie," she responded a tinge of color rising in her cheeks.

"Well that's good to hear because I was hoping we could go to dinner and then work off our meal at the skating rink. Of course, that plan was made before I'd spent an hour running behind a bicycle," he confessed.

"Oh, I am sorry but that won't be possible this evening," she answered.

"May I inquire why not?"

"Certainly," she said with a smile. "I promised Lydia that Addie could spend the night with me. It will be the first time she's stayed over with me, but since tomorrow is Sunday and she doesn't have to go work in the morning, I thought it a splendid plan," she advised.

"Why does Lydia want Addie to spend the night?" he inquired, confused by the turn of events.

"She has a date with Floyd, a salesman she's been keeping company with for some time now. I didn't ask but I got the impression she may be planning on staying out after the curfew and didn't want to take a chance that Addie would give her away. I'm not sure, but she acted as if she were hiding something when she asked me," Tessie explained.

"Do you really think you should be a part of this?" Charlie asked.

"Charlie—I thought we had an agreement," she stated firmly.

"We do, and I think I've been keeping my part of the bargain. I'm not quite so sure you're keeping your eyes open, however," he answered.

"I like having Addie with me. If I felt Lydia were taking advantage of me, I'd call her on it. You know I have no trouble speaking my mind."

"That's a fact, but I can't help thinking there's more going on here than either one of us realize," he answered.

"How would you feel about having dinner here with Addie and me?" she inquired.

"I couldn't refuse that offer," he told her. "I'll expect the two of you to accompany me to the skating rink afterward."

"We'll see," she responded, not sure she was quite up to an evening of skating.

Once dinner was over and the kitchen duties completed by the trio, Charlie knelt down in front of Addie. "How would you like an evening at the skating rink?" he asked the child.

Addie wasn't sure what Charlie was asking since she had never seen a skating rink, but agreed she would be happy to go along. "It's two to one for the skating rink," Charlie told Tessie, pleased he had gotten the upper hand at least once.

"Charlie, I'm not sure I can even stay upright on roller skates. It's been ages since I've tried," she admitted.

"I'll be right at your side, more than happy to hold you up," he bantered, not willing to take no for an answer.

"Get your coat, Addie," he said, motioning to the hall closet. "You, too, Tessie. It will be chilly by the time we return," he informed her.

Addie skipped ahead as the two of them walked toward Charlie's carriage. "I think we better take the buggy. By the time we get through skating, we may be too tired to walk home," Charlie advised laughingly, although Tessie was almost positive he was correct.

☙

Tessie was glad there weren't many people at the skating rink to observe her uncoordinated attempts at the roller skating. Charlie was busy trying to keep Addie upright while Tessie spent the first hour slowly circling while holding onto the railing whenever possible. Soon, Addie was making her way around the rink on her own and Charlie took the opportunity to glide over toward Tessie just as she let go of the railing. His attempt to stabilize her proved an effort in futility. Instead, they both landed on the floor while Addie skated a circle around them.

"Maybe I should give you lessons," the child laughed, gazing down at the couple sprawled on the floor.

Charlie gave her a look of mock indignation as he returned to an upright position and held a hand toward Tessie. "Please, don't pull me down," he chided placing his arm around her waist. After several trips around the rink with Charlie at her side, Tessie decided the skating rink had been an excellent idea.

"Thank you for a wonderful evening, Charlie," Tessie said, bidding him good night at the front door.

"You are more than welcome," he said. Before she knew it, Charlie had gathered her to him, his breath on her cheek. "I think I love you," he said, leaning down and kissing her softly on the lips.

"Charlie, Addie will see you," she reprimanded, avoiding his declaration.

"There's nothing wrong with a young girl seeing two people who care about each other kissing good night," he defended.

"Perhaps not, but it's getting late and I need to get Addie into bed," she told him.

"I'm planning on escorting you to church in the morning, if that's all right?" he asked.

"That will be fine," she answered closing the door. *He loves me,* she thought to herself, walking toward the spare bedroom in a daze.

A noise on the front porch shortly after she had gone to bed, startled Tessie awake. *Probably just a cat knocking over a flower-pot,* she decided and drifted back to sleep.

⋆

The next morning Charlie arrived at ten thirty and was instructed to wait in the parlor while Tessie struggled with the ribbon in Addie's hair.

"I don't know what's wrong this morning," she said aloud. "Nothing seems to be getting completed on schedule. We'd better get going or we'll be late," she told Charlie. "Just let me get our coats."

"This letter was in the door when I arrived," Charlie told her as she and Addie passed through the parlor on their way to the hall closet.

"Just leave it on the table. I'll read it after church," she replied, pinning her hat in place.

"Would you like to eat at the Harvey House?" Charlie invited as they walked toward church.

"I'd love to, but I'd like to stop off at the house first and read that letter you discovered. My curiosity's beginning to get the best of me."

"Not at all," he said, each of them grasping one of Addie's hands as she skipped along between them.

Tessie and Addie had become regulars at church and Charlie was always with them on the Sundays he was in Florence. Addie made a few friends, but remained most comfortable sitting between the two of them, leaning her head on Charlie's arm.

"Where did summer go, Charlie?" Tessie asked as they reached the house. "It seems only yesterday I was tending my roses, and now winter is almost upon us," she said, pulling her collar tighter.

"They say that's what happens when you get older. You lose all sense of time," he teased, opening the front door.

"We're going out to dinner shortly, Addie, so please stay neat," Tessie told the youngster who nodded in agreement.

Tessie sat down on the sofa and tore open the envelope, quickly scanning the letter. Automatically her eyes looked toward Addie who was sitting in the rocking chair stitching on her quilt. She handed the letter to Charlie, who slowly read the contents.

> *Dear Dr. Wilshire,*
>
> *Floyd and me ran away and are getting married. Floyd says we can't afford to take Addie 'cause I won't be working since I'm going to have a baby. Anyways, I didn't know what to do about Addie and since she spends most of her spare time with you, I decided you could just have her. I left all her things at the hotel and maybe she could just keep working there like usual. It would keep her out of your way in the mornings most days. In*

case you don't want her around, maybe you could
find some orphanage or something. Hope you
don't get too angry about this but I got my own
life to live.

Yours truly,
Lydia

"How are you going to tell her?" he asked sympathetically.

"I'm not sure," Tessie answered, glad that he didn't say, "I told you so." Lydia hadn't fooled Charlie, not for a minute.

"Do you want to be alone with Addie while you tell her, or would you like me to stay?" he asked.

"Please don't leave. I need all the help I can get with this," she answered, feeling desperately inadequate.

"I'm hungry. Are we going to eat now?" Addie called.

"Come here, Addie I need to talk to you," Tessie responded, holding her hand out toward the youngster.

Addie slid onto Tessie's lap. "What?" she inquired when Tessie said nothing.

"When Charlie arrived this morning, he found a letter in the door. It's from Lydia," she began.

"Why did Lydia write you a letter? She can just walk over and talk to you. That was silly, wasn't it?"

"She wrote the letter because it was easier than talking to us. Last night Lydia and Floyd went away to get married," Tessie explained.

"When is she coming back?" the child asked, her eyes wide with surprise.

"She's not planning on coming back right away. She and Floyd are going to live in another town, but Lydia has agreed that you can stay with me. It makes me very happy that she's going to allow you to live here," Tessie concluded as enthusiastically as possible, hoping to soften the message.

"I guess she must love Floyd more than me," Addie responded. "Do you think she'll ever want to see me again?" she asked, her voice quivering.

"Lydia loves you very much and I'm sure she'll be back one day to see you. It's just that she's ready to start a new life with Floyd and thought you'd be better off here," Tessie replied, pulling the child closer and issuing a silent prayer for guidance.

Suddenly, Addie pushed herself away. "When you and Charlie get married, who are you going to leave me with?" the child asked, looking back and forth between the couple.

"You would live with us, wouldn't she, Tess?" Charlie quickly responded, ignoring Tessie's reproving look.

"Charlie and I don't have plans to get married," she explained.

"But when we do, we'll tell you right away. We would want you to live with us when that happens," Charlie stated.

"We'll discuss this later," Tessie told him, when Addie was looking away.

Disregarding her comment, he gained Addie's attention. "Are you still hungry?"

"Yes," she responded dejectedly.

"Well, then I think we should be on our way to the Harvey House. Maybe, we'll have some chocolate layer cake for dessert," he added, watching as Addie gave him a fleeting smile.

"She'll be all right," Charlie informed Tessie. "With our love and God's help, things will work out."

"I know. . .'All things work for good to those who love the Lord.' I'm just not sure Addie knows that."

seven

November arrived bringing several inches of snow and frigid temperatures. Charlie, Tessie, and Addie were well-bundled as they left the Opera House, their stomachs overly full. It had been a splendid Thanksgiving dinner and the Opera House had served as an excellent community dining room for the annual feast.

"Mr. Banion. . .Dr. Wilshire, come quick! There's a fire at the depot and a couple of people are hurt pretty bad," came the cry of Lawrence MacAfee, racing toward them on his large stallion.

"Let me take your horse," Charlie ordered. "Take Dr. Wilshire to her house. She'll need to get her medical bag. Check to see if your wife is willing to come over to Dr. Wilshire's and look after Addie. We may be a while."

Instructions issued, Charlie urged the horse into full gallop toward the railroad yard.

Tessie rapidly checked her black bag, adding several salves, clean sheets, and bandages. Confident she had those items she might need to aid any victims, she hurried back to the carriage. Lawrence and Addie sat patiently waiting, eyes riveted toward the heavy smoke spiraling ever upward, casting a smoggy glow over the surrounding area.

Tessie had barely made it into the carriage when Mr. MacAfee snapped the reins commanding the horses into action, throwing both passengers backward against the seat. The horses scarcely had an opportunity to reach their speed when Lawrence pulled back on the reins, bringing them to an abrupt halt not far from the station.

"I'd better not get the horses any closer to the fire or they'll spook on us, Doc. I'll take the little gal home and be back to help just as quick as a wink," he said, giving Addie a reassuring grin.

Tessie didn't bother to reply, her mind now fully focused toward the task at hand. It appeared that total chaos reigned throughout the area until she made her way a bit closer. Charlie had strategically placed himself in the midst of activity, shouting orders and assembling men in bucket brigades to douse the flames from every possible angle and as quickly as humanly possible. Spotting Tessie, he motioned her toward him while continuing his command post, mindful of each new sputter of flames threatening to ignite out of control.

"We've moved the injured to the depot. The fire broke out in one of the passenger cars. I'm not sure what happened, but it looks like there are only a few people needing medical care."

"If you keep pushing your men at this rate, you'll have me caring for a lot more," Tessie reprimanded him. "They need to trade off. Move some of the men that are closest to the fire farther back down the line and switch them about frequently. Otherwise, they'll drop from heat exhaustion," she ordered.

He smiled at the brusqueness of her order, but knew she was right. He should have thought about that himself! Immediately, he ordered the last ten men to exchange places with the first ten, while he watched Tessie hurry off toward the train station. He smiled as she stopped momentarily to check the hand of a firefighter, then motioned him to follow her into the depot. *That's quite a woman,* he thought, and then quickly forced his mind back to the conflagration, knowing that any stir of wind could impede their progress.

Tessie entered the station and found there were only three patients awaiting her, not counting the unwilling young man she had forced from duty.

"It appears you're all doing fairly well without my assistance," she said, giving them a bright smile, which quickly faded upon hearing the muffled groans from the other side of the room.

Her eyes darted toward the sound, just as one of the men offered, "That one over there, he's hurt pretty bad. I'm not sure how it happened, but it looks like he's got a few broken bones."

"Do you know who he is?" she inquired, walking around the wooden benches toward the injured man.

"He was a passenger that came into town on the train earlier. One of our men went over to the Harvey House looking for volunteers for the bucket brigade—don't think he had been on the fire line long before collapsing. Charlie had him down the line quite a ways since he wasn't a railroader. Besides, he was dressed in those fancy duds."

"Are the rest of you all right for now?" she inquired, kneeling beside the man.

"Sure thing, Doc. We would have stayed out there, but Charlie wouldn't hear of it. Heat got to us but we ain't burnt or nothing. Okay with you if we head back out?"

"Stick around a little longer. At least until I get a good look at this gentleman. I may need some help. Besides, I think they can do without you a little longer," she responded, knowing that wasn't the answer they wanted to hear.

It didn't take more than a quick glance to know she was going to need help. "Get some water on to boil and if there's no water, melt some snow, lots of it. I'm going to need all of you to help in just a little while, so don't take off," she ordered, taking command of the situation.

Coming back toward the patient she noted the pain reflected in his dark brown eyes. His lips were in a tight, straight line making them almost nonexistent and he had turned ashen-gray. As Tessie surveyed the situation, she was grateful to see someone had placed a make-shift tourniquet around the upper leg to stop any excessive bleeding. It had done the job. A brief hand to his forehead proved there was little or no fever.

"I'm Dr. Wilshire and hopefully we're going to have you fixed up in a short while," she said, giving him her best smile.

"I'd be thankful if you could do that," he responded through clenched teeth, watching as she walked toward the stove at the end of the room.

Quickly she surveyed the men and finding the most muscular appearing of the group, quietly inquired, "Have you got a strong stomach or are you given to fainting at the sight of blood and pain?"

"I can hold out with the best of 'em," he stated proudly, not sure what he was getting himself into.

"Ever seen your wife give birth or helped set a bone? Ever watched while someone had a cut sewn?" she fired at him.

"Been there to help when all my younguns was born—my wife does the hard part. I just pray and help the babe along when it gets time. Don't know that I've ever seen much else, but I grew up on the farm and helped with the sick animals a lot," he answered, not sure what she was wanting him to do.

"Have you ever fainted?" she asked, beginning to scrub her hands and arms in the hot water.

"No, ma'am. Ain't never fainted."

"Good. Scrub yourself," she commanded.

"Excuse me, ma'am, did you say scrub?"

"That's right. Get a bucket of that hot water and begin scrubbing. Watch how I do it. I want your hands clean as the day you were born, so you better get busy. By the way, what's your name?" she asked, giving him a quick smile.

"It's Alexander Thurston. Call me Alex," he responded.

"Pleased to meet you, Alex, and I appreciate your willingness to become my assistant," she replied, grinning at the look of dismay that passed across the man's face at that remark.

"As soon as we get through washing I want you other men to throw out the water and pour some for yourselves. Each one of you scrub yourselves the same way we have. Make sure you take your time and get good and clean," she ordered.

None of them even thought to defy her command, each nodding in agreement as though it were commonplace for this young woman doctor to give them directives. They stood staring after her as she turned and walked back to the grimacing man on the floor.

Pulling one of the sterilized and carefully wrapped packets from her bag, Tessie produced a pair of scissors and began cutting away the remainder of the pant leg. Once removed, she found fragments of the broken leg at an unwieldy angle to his body. Nerves, bone, skin, and other debris protruded from the wound, banishing Tessie's hope the repair would be easy.

"I need to clean the wound and then we'll begin to get you put back together," Tessie told the man.

"I don't believe anybody here knows your name. You feel up to talking just a little?" she asked, hoping to keep his mind otherwise occupied while she probed the gash.

"Name's Edward Buford. I'm here visiting from England. My sister lives in Chicago and I had been there to visit with her. Thought I'd see a bit more of the country before returning home," he told her, attempting to keep from yelping in pain as she carefully continued cleaning the leg.

"I thought I detected an English accent earlier," she remarked. "I am sorry you've met with accident in our country. Especially at a time when you were acting as a good-will ambassador, helping put out the fire," she continued. "How did this happen? The men tell me you were at the end of the line and apparently no one saw the accident occur."

"It was a bizarre accident. A runaway team of horses pulling a loaded wagon went out of control and was headed right for me. I tried to jump out of the way and twisted my leg as I fell," he began.

"That couldn't have caused an injury this severe," she interrupted.

"No. I was unable to move quickly enough and the wagon ran over my leg. Then, as if to add insult to injury, the horses reared which caused the wagon to tip over. I was fortunate enough to have the wagon land elsewhere, but a large barrel landed on top of my injured leg. That would account for any corn meal you may find hidden away in that leg," he advised, trying to make light of his condition.

"I appreciate that bit of information, Mr. Buford," she responded with a smile. "I'm going to wash out the wound. The water may be a little warm but we need to get this leg cleansed.

"Alex, I'd appreciate it if you would keep the basin emptied and bring me hot water as needed," she instructed, noting the recently initiated assistant seemed to be bearing up to the ministrations thus far.

Tessie repeatedly poured hot water over the wound, irrigating it into a basin positioned beneath the leg, with Alex assisting her as they turned Mr. Buford, permitting access from all angles. Her patient's lips once again formed a tight line and his eyes closed securely with each new movement or the rush of water. A low groan emitted when she gave a final dousing of the area with iodine.

Looking toward the three men who had been busy scrubbing themselves, she noted all of them with the exception of one seemed up to the job at hand. Gathering them around, she dismissed the young man who looked as though he would pass out at any moment, and then explained to the remainder how she was going to pull the bone back into Mr. Buford's leg and then position it to join together. They needed to retract the bone far enough to ease it into position, which would require all of them working together. Carefully she explained where each of them should stand and exactly what they were to do when she issued the orders, making them individually repeat the instructions, wanting to feel assured each knew his duty.

Returning to Mr. Buford, she leaned over him and took his hand. "Sir, I need to set your leg and since it will be a rather painful procedure, unless you object, I am going to give you some anesthetic to knock you out for a short period of time," she explained.

"Dr. Wilshire, had I known you had ether with you, I would have requested it an hour ago and foregone the pain of you cleansing my wound," he said, giving her a weak smile.

"I take that to mean we may proceed, Mr. Buford."

"As quickly as possible, my dear woman, and feel free to knock me out for more than just a few minutes," he replied as she placed a pad with the drops of ether over his nose.

"Quickly gentlemen, let's take our positions and get to work," she called out as soon as the anesthetic had taken effect.

Uttering a fleeting prayer that God guide them, Tessie called out the orders, "Pull, twist right, relax, pull twist left, relax." Finally, they had the leg aligned to her exacting specifications and sat watching while she carefully sewed the wound, with the exception of Alex. He continued to anticipate her needs and fetch items until she completed the operation.

"You've been a very able assistant, Alex. I appreciate all you've done to help and if ever there's anything I can do for you or your family, I hope you'll call upon me."

"Was my pleasure, ma'am. Wait 'til I tell the missus I helped with a real operation. She'll never believe it."

"Well if she doesn't, you have her come and see me the next time she's in town and I'll tell her just what a wonderful job you did," she assured him.

Just as Mr. Buford was beginning to regain consciousness, Charlie walked into the station. "We've finally got the fire out," he announced, taking in the scene of men with rolled-up sleeves gathered around Tessie and her patient.

"How are things going in here?" he inquired.

"We're making progress," she answered. "Mr. Buford's leg has been set and as soon as we get some splints on it, I believe we'll be finished."

"I'll take care of that, Doc. I know where there's some pieces of wood that would work real good," responded one of the men who had assisted in setting the leg.

"Thank you," she called after the disappearing young man. "You look as though you could use a basin of water and a little rest yourself, Charlie."

"That's an understatement," he confided, settling onto one of the wooden benches close at hand. "Tell me about your patient," he requested, indicating the groggy form of Mr. Buford.

Sitting down beside him, she wrung out a clean cloth in the basin of water Alex brought to her. Reaching toward him, she sponged the soot and ash off his face and dipping the cloth back in the water once again began rinsing.

"Thought I better get a few layers of that soot off and make sure it was really you I was talking to," she joked. "My patient is Edward Buford. He's here visiting from England. He tells me he had been to Chicago visiting his sister and before departing decided to see a little more of America. I gather he knows no one in the area. Since he must stay off that leg, I'll need to find some accommodations for him."

"I think Mr. Vance would agree the railroad should provide him a room at the Harvey House since he was helping with the fire. I'll see if I can get one on the first floor. Otherwise, I'll make other arrangements," he assured her.

"Will these work for splints, Doc?" the young man inquired, walking through the front door, proud of his find.

"Those will be wonderful," she beamed at him. "Bring them over and we'll finish this job."

"I'll go check about a room at the Harvey House while you finish," Charlie told her.

"Good," she replied and moved toward her patient. "Alex, give us a hand, would you?" Together they placed the wooden splints on either side of the leg and bound them in place.

"That's about all we can do," she told the men. "I'd appreciate it if several of you would remain to help move Mr. Buford. Charlie should be back shortly," she advised.

Checking his vital signs, she was pleased to find they were normal. "Mr. Buford, I'm afraid you're going to be required to remain in our fair city for a period of time. I'm hopeful you'll walk without a limp if you follow instructions and remain off the leg as long as I deem necessary," she told him, not sure what his reaction would be to this change of plans.

"After you've worked so diligently to make me whole again, how could I fail to follow your prescribed instructions?" he asked, a woozy smile on his face.

"Everything's arranged at the Harvey House," Charlie announced, coming through the front door of the station. "I've explained he's had an injury and they're expecting him."

"Thank you, Charlie. Men, if you'd carefully lift Mr. Buford onto one of the benches, I believe we can carry him over to the Harvey House" she instructed.

"Don't worry, ma'am. We'll carry him as if he were a babe," Alex assured her as they gently lifted Mr. Buford onto the bench. "You just walk along side and give a holler if we're doing anything to cause him pain," he instructed the young doctor.

Upon their arrival at the Harvey House, the entourage was met by Mrs. Winter. Resembling a drum major in the Fourth of July parade, she led the procession down the hall to the designated room. Tessie stood back and allowed the matron to remain in charge until it was time to move Mr. Buford onto the bed. Mrs. Winter's cheeks visibly colored at the praise Tessie heaped upon her.

"I believe you've won Mrs. Winter's allegiance," Charlie whispered to Tessie as the men carefully placed Mr. Buford on the bed.

"That was my intent. I want my patient to receive excellent care while he's residing here. The best way to insure that is through Mrs. Winter. Don't you agree?" she whispered back.

Charlie leaned his head back and laughed delightedly at her response.

"Mr. Banion! You're going to have to keep your voice

down if you want to remain in this room. Just think what damage could have occurred if your rowdiness startled Mr. Buford and caused him to twist that leg," Mrs. Winter reprimanded, hands on hips and eyes shooting looks of disapproval.

"Yes, ma'am," Charlie replied, giving her a salute while backing from the room and trying to keep from doubling over in laughter. "I'll meet you outside," Charlie loudly whispered to Tessie, peeking his head around the door jamb and then quickly receding when Mrs. Winter started toward him.

"Thank you all for your able assistance and now, if I could have a few moments alone with my patient, I believe he'll soon be ready for a good night of sleep," Tessie said to the gathered assistants.

As they filed out of the room, Tessie stopped Mrs. Winter. "I'd appreciate it if you'd remain, Mrs. Winter. Since you'll be in charge of the day-to-day care of Mr. Buford, I'd like you to hear my instructions." Mrs. Winter once again took on the cloak of self-import as she ushered the delegation from the room and then returned to Mr. Buford's bedside, hands folded in front of her, prepared for instruction.

"You'll be pleased to know, Dr. Wilshire, that I've had previous experience nursing the infirm," Mrs. Winter offered.

"That does please me," Tessie responded, smiling at the woman and then her patient. "Mr. Buford is visiting from England and I am hopeful we can show him not only the best of medical care, but the fine hospitality of our country while he's required to be bedfast. Mr. Banion located his trunk and I feel certain he has all necessary items with him. Mr. Banion has requested if Mr. Buford needs anything, the purchases be placed on his bill and presented to the railroad," she explained.

"I'm hopeful there is a strong young man working for you that is able to follow instruction and can assist Mr. Buford daily with bathing and dressing. With his leg splinted, it will present some special problems and I certainly don't want him to bear weight on that leg for a period of time," Tessie explained.

"I know just the young man," Mrs. Winter declared. "I'll go and get him right now," and off she bustled, ready to fulfill the first order of her mission.

Once Mrs. Winter was out of earshot, Mr. Buford looked at Tessie and inquired, with a slight twinkle in his eyes, "How long am I to be held hostage?"

"I'm not sure how long it will take you to heal. You've had a serious injury. If you do well, perhaps after a short period we can put you on a train back to Chicago and you can finish recuperating with your sister and her family. Would that bolster your spirits a bit?"

"I suppose so, but it would appear the time I envisioned seeing the country shall be spent looking out a window," he replied, trying to keep a pleasant frame of mind. "Don't misunderstand—I am truly grateful for your excellent medical attention, doctor, and if you'll agree to continue treating me, I'll attempt to be a good patient."

"I can't ask for much more than that, Mr. Buford," Tessie responded as Mrs. Winter and a muscular young man of about eighteen entered the room.

Tessie carefully instructed both the young man and Mrs. Winter in the necessary care of Mr. Buford's injury. Bidding the three of them good night, she assured Edward she would check on him in the morning.

Wearily she exited the front door and found Charlie leaning against the porch railing. "Did you get Mrs. Winter organized?" he inquired.

"I believe she'll do just fine," Tessie answered as they walked down the front steps.

"You look exhausted," Charlie remarked, lifting a wisp of hair that had worked it's way out of her ribbon, carefully tucking it behind her ear.

"It's been a long evening," she replied. "I feel as though I could sleep for a week," she admitted.

When they had completed the short walk to her front door, Charlie leaned forward and enveloped her in his arms, allowing her head to rest upon his chest. He stroked her hair and held her close for just a few moments and then lifted her face toward his, placing a soft kiss upon her lips.

"I'm glad you've come into my life, Dr. Tessie Wilshire," he whispered to her and then pulled her in a tight embrace and kissed her thoroughly.

"I'm glad too," she answered, smiling up at him, "but I think we'd both better get some rest," she added.

"That's the doctor in you—always being practical," he said, giving her a broad smile. "I'll leave you now if you'll promise to stop at the station in the morning so we can have breakfast. Do you want me to check on Addie for you?" he inquired.

"Oh good heavens, how could I forget Addie?" she exclaimed sheepishly. "I'd better get her," she continued.

"Why don't I just stop over at the MacAfees. She's probably already asleep. They'll enjoy having her and you need to get to bed," he ordered.

"If you think they won't mind. Tell Mrs. MacAfee I'll be by first thing in the morning," she conceded.

Placing one last kiss on her cheek, Charlie bounded off the porch and back toward the station to get his horse and ride to the MacAfee.

❧

In the days that followed, Tessie diligently visited her new patient, pleased with his progress. She had begun making her visits to Mr. Buford in the late afternoon after completing office hours. Tessie enjoyed the daily visits, not only because her medical treatment was proving effective, but because Mr. Buford was an entertaining and knowledgeable companion. Addie would walk with her to the hotel and then head for the kitchen, anxious to see the chef and taste his inventive recipes. On this particular day Tessie knew John would not be in the kitchen until later, since he had gone to make a special purchase of oysters.

"Come along, Addie, you can meet Mr. Buford," Tessie instructed, helping Addie remove her new winter hat and coat.

Addie nodded agreement, although it was evident she would be off and running the minute John returned.

"Now who might this fine young woman be?" Mr. Buford inquired as Addie followed Tessie into the room.

"This is Addie Baker. She lives with me and if you care to converse with her, you'll need to be sure she is looking directly at you. She's deaf," Tessie explained.

"Come here, young woman," Mr. Buford instructed while patting the side of the bed. "Come close so we can talk."

Tessie sat down in the rocking chair and nodded to Addie as the child cautiously approached Edward's bedside. Amazed at his ability to charm the young girl, Tessie sat mesmerized for almost an hour while he entertained the youngster. Several times Tessie was sure he had attempted to sign with Addie but, not wanting to disrupt the developing rapport, she remained silent throughout their conversation, surprised he had little difficulty understanding the child's occasional distorted words.

John's appearance outside the hotel snapped Addie out

of her reverie and with a hasty wave of the arm, she was off the edge of the bed and out of the room.

"I apologize, Mr. Buford. I'm afraid Addie's first love is being in the kitchen with John," Tessie stated. "That's not meant as an excuse for her rudeness, but rather an explanation," she continued, shaking her head in mock exasperation.

"No explanations or excuses necessary," he responded laughingly. "She's a delightful child. By the way, do you recall that you've promised to call me Edward on several occasions?"

"Now that you mention it, I do remember. I'll try and do better in the future," she answered, picking up her medical bag and moving closer to the bedside.

"Would you be offended if I asked a few questions?"

"About Addie? Not at all," she answered.

"Well, about Addie and you," he countered.

"I suppose you can ask so long as I may retain the right not to answer," she offered.

"Fair enough! How did Addie come to live with you? Is she a relative?"

"No, we're not related," she stated and then, reminiscing, explained how she had met Addie and Lydia along with the subsequent chain of events that had bonded them together.

"My heartfelt desire is that I can provide Addie with the necessary tools to prepare her for the future. I've prayed earnestly about her deafness for I'm sure life will be difficult unless she is equipped to meet many challenges."

"Do you know what caused her deafness?" he inquired.

"Her sister told me she was able to hear up until about a year ago. That was as much information as I was able to glean from her. Lydia, Addie's sister, was extremely jealous of any attention the child received and when I questioned about Addie she became infuriated. Consequently, I have very limited knowledge. I noticed you attempting to sign with her, didn't I?" Tessie asked as she finished checking her patient's vital signs and began to unwrap his leg to check the stitches.

"Yes, you did. My niece was deaf and I learned to sign in order to better communicate with her several years ago when they came to England," he told her, watching as she carefully removed the bandages from his wound.

"You say she was deaf. Is she deceased?"

"Oh no, not at all. I've just come from visiting her at my sister's home in Chicago. She's had surgery and is now able to hear That's why I inquired about Addie's loss of hearing," he explained.

A chill of excitement traveled up Tessie's spine at hearing his words. Her fingers ceased their movement and she looked directly into his eyes. "I want to know everything about this surgery. How much can you tell me?" she asked, obviously impatient for answers.

"Not any of the technicalities, I'm afraid. My brother-in-law performed the surgery. While he and Juliette, my sister, were in England two years ago, he heard of a surgeon in Germany who was performing surgery to correct deafness with some success. He left Juliette and Genevive with our family in England and traveled to meet with the doctor in Germany. He remained in Germany for almost a year, studying and developing the technique. The success rate has been very limited but for some, like Genevive, hearing is fully restored," he explained.

Tessie's mind whirled with the information she was receiving. Perhaps there was hope for Addie to hear again. Perhaps this surgery was the answer!

Carefully she removed the sutures and then wrapped the splints back in place. "How can I find out more?" she asked, closing her medical bag and pulling the rocking chair close to his bedside.

"You could send an inquiry to my brother-in-law. I'd be happy to write a letter of introduction you could enclose with it. I should have written them of my whereabouts before now, anyway. This will force me to take up my pen," he told her.

"Oh Edward, would you do that? I'd be so grateful," she replied, clasping his hand between both of hers.

Lifting her hand, he lightly kissed it before she could pull away. "It will be my pleasure," he answered, holding onto her hand for a brief moment longer.

Tessie felt her face flush and hoped Edward would think it was from her excitement over the surgical prospects rather than from his kiss.

"I really must be leaving," she announced. "I'm going to write a letter to your brother-in-law this evening, Edward. I'd appreciate it if you wouldn't mention this to anyone yet. If it turns out Addie isn't able to have the surgery, it will be less explaining."

"I understand," he replied, "and I'll honor your wishes, but I have a good feeling about this."

"So do I. I'll see you tomorrow," she answered, slipping into her gray double-breasted wool coat before heading off in search of Addie.

eight

Although writing a letter to Edward's brother-in-law immediately after dinner was Tessie's intent, her resolve melted at the beckoning look of the young child holding out a needle and thread. Addie was determined to have her quilt completed before Christmas, notwithstanding the fact everyone told her she had set an unobtainable goal.

"I'll sew for a little while, but then I must write a letter," Tessie said, reaching out to take the already threaded needle Addie offered. "I wrote and told Aunt Phiney you were making a quilt. I even sent some little pieces of the fabric for her to see."

"Did she like it?" Addie inquired.

"Very much. In fact, when I received her letter the other day she said she was sending you colored thread to match the cloth. She suggested perhaps you could weave the thread together to sew the binding and it would be very pretty. What do you think?"

"Three colors woven together would be beautiful," Addie answered, as Tessie began sewing, Stitching effortlessly, Tessie found herself watching Addie, thinking that perhaps one day soon the young girl would be able to hear.

Addie looked up and smiled as she pulled her needle through the layers of fabric. "You're not sewing, you're daydreaming," Addie chided.

"Addie, what would you think if I told you that maybe, just maybe, there's an operation that would restore your hearing?" Tessie asked, leaning forward, her eyes riveted on the youngster.

"You know I want to be a doctor like you, so that would be wonderful," the child responded. "Would the operation hurt a lot?"

"It would probably hurt some, I'm not sure just how much. I shouldn't have even brought this up. I don't even know if it's possible, but Edward told me about his niece. She had this operation and now she can hear. So, you see, I'd like to find out more about it—to see if you could get that same kind of help," she concluded.

"We shouldn't get too hopeful," Addie responded, taking over in an adult fashion, while Tessie seemed more the excited child.

"You're right," Tessie said, smiling. "We'll not talk about it any further until I have more information, but I'll be praying about it and you do the same," she counseled Addie.

Praying that evening, Tessie felt a surge of excitement. She knew this was God's plan to restore Addie's hearing and she was going to see it to fruition. The added medical expertise she might glean would be an added bonus. Leaning down, she placed a kiss on Addie's cheek, tucked her into bed for the night, and carefully penned a letter to Dr. Byron Lundstrom. "No wonder I'm so tired," she mused, clicking open the watch pinned to her bodice. It was near midnight.

❧

Working through her schedule the next morning, Tessie's thoughts wandered, delighting in the possibilities that lay ahead. She was anxious for noon to arrive, her concentration waning as the morning slowly progressed.

I hope he has his letter written, she thought, just as her last patient was leaving.

"Do you know of a doctor and little girl who might be

interested in lunch at the Harvey House?" Charlie asked as he sauntered into the office, admiring how fresh and lovely she could look after a morning of seeing ill patients.

"Oh, I don't think I can today, Charlie. I need to see Edward before my first appointment this afternoon," she responded apologetically, continuing to bustle around the office assuring everything was in order for her next patient.

"Edward? Would that be Mr. Buford?"

"Yes," she responded, without further explanation.

"The last I knew you were addressing him as Mr. Buford. When did you and Mr. Buford begin addressing each other on a first-name basis?" he inquired, his thick eyebrows raised in speculation.

"Why, he requested I call him by his first name shortly after I began treating him," she answered, surprised at the tone Charlie had taken

"Are you now on a first-name basis with all your patients?" he countered, irritated she felt comfortable enough with this stranger to be so familiar.

"You're acting childish," she retorted. "I don't have time to stand and bicker over such a petty matter. I really must get to the Harvey House," she stated, tucking the letter into her handbag. "I need to get Addie so, if you'll excuse me, I'll be on my way," she said, moving toward his tall figure which was blocking the doorway.

"Let's get Addie. We can all go to the Harvey House, see Mr. Buford, and then have lunch," he suggested, sure he had found a solution that would force her to accept his invitation.

"You're welcome to walk along with us, but once I see Edward there are other errands I need to complete," she responded, pushing past him into the parlor where the child sat playing with a doll house Uncle Jon had constructed and sent to her.

"You have to eat lunch sometime, so I'll just tag along until the two of you are ready and then I'll join you," he replied with a grin, feeling sure she would succumb to his offer.

Handing Addie her white fur muff, they walked the short distance to the Harvey House. "I'll take Addie to the kitchen," Charlie offered, upon their arrival.

"No, it's better if she comes with me. The kitchen will be in chaos with the noon rush and she'll be in the way," she answered, placing an arm around Addie's shoulder and maneuvering her down the hallway.

"Sounds as if you're in charge," Charlie said, watching while Addie and Tessie went directly to Edward's room.

"This is a pleasant surprise," Edward stated as the two of them entered his room. "I was expecting Mrs. White with a lunch tray and instead I see the two prettiest women in all of Kansas," he complimented, with a large smile.

"Thank you for your kind words," Tessie replied. "I was wondering if possibly you'd had an opportunity to write your brother-in-law," she inquired meekly.

"Ah, so it's not me you're interested in, but rather my brother-in-law. He's a happily married man and you'd be much better off with me. I'm of a better temperament, and considerably more lovable," he teased.

Tessie felt her face flush and was glad Addie was looking out the window and hadn't been privy to Edward's words.

"I wanted to. . .I mean I was hoping. . .I thought perhaps," she stammered.

"Out with it woman, just what is it you want? Love, money, my family name? Don't hesitate, it's yours for the asking," he jested, causing her embarrassment but enjoying it too much to stop.

"Edward! Someone will hear you and take your words seriously," she reprimanded. "I came early to inquire if you'd written to your brother-in-law because I wanted to post the letters before the mail leaves on the afternoon train," she advised, her decorum now fully intact.

"I see," he responded somberly, stroking his chin. "So you thought I'd have a letter written to Byron by noon today, knowing I haven't written since I departed their home?" he asked, eyeing her in mock seriousness.

"I was hopeful," she responded plaintively, suddenly realizing his zeal would not be the same caliber as hers. After all, he had only met Addie yesterday!

Seeing the dejected look in her eyes, he quit bantering, reached under his pillow and pulled out a sheet of paper, holding it up for her to see.

"Do you suppose this would do?" he asked.

"Oh, Edward, thank you," she replied.

"There's only one requirement," he told her stoically.

"What's that," she asked, her tone serious.

"You'll have to come over here and get it," he answered with a grin.

As she approached the bed he quickly moved the letter into his left hand. Just as she leaned forward to retrieve the epistle, he raised up, meeting her lips with a soft, gentle kiss.

"I know I shouldn't have done that," he said, lying back on his pillows.

"You're right! You shouldn't have and if you weren't in that bed, I'd have your hide," Charlie bellowed from doorway.

"Charlie, please! There's no need for that kind of talk and I'd appreciate it if you'd keep your voice down. We don't need to alert everyone in the hotel that you're unhappy," Tessie scolded in a hushed voice.

"I don't know why you're upset with me! You should be putting him in his place," he replied angrily.

"Why don't you take Addie and wait outside. We can discuss this privately when you've calmed down," she suggested, hopeful he wouldn't cause a further scene.

"Fine. Addie and I will wait outside—outside his door, not outside the hotel," he responded, giving Edward a final glare as he took Addie's hand.

"I'm sorry. I didn't realize you were promised to Mr. Banion," he stated apologetically.

"You need not apologize in that regard. Mr. Banion and I are not promised. We've been enjoying each other's company since I arrived in Florence. I do not, however, belong to anyone," she responded, angry at Charlie for his possessive attitude. "I would, however, be willing to accept your apology for kissing me without permission," she added.

"I'm afraid I could never apologize for kissing you. It gave me too much pleasure," he stated emphatically, a smile playing on his lips as he handed her the letter.

"Thank you for this," she stated, looking at the letter in her hand.

"My pleasure. I hope it will bring happiness to you. I'm afraid it's already brought unhappiness to Mr. Banion," he replied.

"I'd better leave now. I'll be back to check your leg around four o'clock," she told him, placing his letter in her handbag with the one she had written.

He lifted his hand in a wave as she left the room, pleased she would be returning later in the day.

Walking into the hallway, Tessie quickly retrieved Addie's hand, walked directly past Charlie and out of the hotel without uttering a word. She was acutely aware of

Charlie's footsteps directly behind her as she marched toward the post office, and had almost reached the door when he took hold of her arm.

"Are you planning on walking all over town to avoid discussing this matter with me?" he questioned.

"I have a letter I must mail immediately. After that I will talk with you, but please don't assume that I have an obligation to discuss my personal life with you, Charlie," she responded.

He felt as though he had been slapped in the face. She was actually angry with him when that presumptuous foreigner should be the one receiving her wrath. He didn't understand her attitude, but wanting some form of explanation, he waited outside the post office while she posted her letters and then moved alongside Addie when they exited the building.

Addie slipped her small gloved hand into Charlie's larger one. She didn't know all the words that had been spoken, but it was obvious Charlie and Tessie were arguing. The air crackled with animosity. Peeking up at Charlie from under the brim of her small hat, she felt a hint of reassurance when he gave her a quick wink and squeezed her hand. Tessie wasn't looking anywhere but straight ahead, and Charlie noted her face remained etched in a frown.

"I'm going to my room," Addie announced, shedding her coat as they walked in the front door, wanting no part of the dissension.

"Addie needs to eat lunch and I have only a short time before my next patient arrives," Tessie remarked avoiding his eyes.

"I'm not going to be the cause of Addie missing her lunch. Can you reschedule your next patient?" he cautiously inquired.

"No, I can't. I don't expect a patient to be inconvenienced by my personal problems," she replied, moving toward the kitchen.

"Perhaps it would be best if I came back later in the day when we've both had time to give this matter some thought. I could be back about four o'clock if that would be acceptable to you," Charlie offered.

"I must return to check Edward's leg at four o'clock," she answered, continuing to prepare lunch.

Charlie felt the blood begin to rise in his neck and then up his face. Edward again! He was glad Tessie wasn't looking at him. Attempting to gain control before speaking, he turned his back and took several deep breaths. A further outburst might cause irreconcilable differences and he didn't want that to occur.

"Do you know what time you'll return? I could come by after your visit or after dinner, if you prefer," he asked, his words spoken in a soft precise manner.

"After dinner would be better, I believe," Tessie responded, setting two places at the table.

"Since it appears I'm not invited to lunch, I'll be back at seven o'clock," he stated, trying to lighten the mood.

When she didn't answer, he backed out the doorway and left the house, not sure how a simple invitation to lunch had turned into such a disaster.

For Tessie, the day quickly passed. She had several physicals for new railroad employees as well as ailing townsfolk with a variety of complaints. By four o'clock she had seen her last patient and she and Addie were on their way back to the Harvey House, both bundled against the declining temperature and cold winds.

"Could I go see John in the kitchen?" Addie requested, as they grew closer to the hotel. Tessie smiled and gave her permission, aware the day's events had been stressful not only for her and Charlie, but for Addie as well.

"Looks like my patient has taken on his own course of treatment," she stated, seeing Edward sitting in a chair with his leg propped on a stool.

"I promise I didn't place any weight on the leg. John and one of the other cooks helped move me. Mrs. Winter took pity on me when I complained of lying in bed all day, and came back with the two men to help me into the chair. However, if it means you'll cease being my physician, I'll return to bed and not move an inch until ordered," he answered, giving her a charming smile.

"I'm sure it will do no harm. I had planned to make arrangements for you to be up in a chair by tomorrow anyway. I must say, you certainly seem to have captivated Mrs. Winter. She's generally not so accommodating," Tessie advised, as she began unwrapping the leg.

"So I've been told by any number of people. Perhaps it's my accent," he offered.

"Perhaps, but most likely it's your flattery that's turned her head," she surmised.

"Flattery? And here I thought it was my perfect English and extraordinary good looks," he teased.

"I'm sure that's helped also," she affirmed, noting his well chiseled features, sandy hair, and twinkling blue eyes, which seemed to laugh at her.

"And have I turned your head, Dr. Tessie Wilshire?" he asked, lifting her chin so their eyes would meet.

Tessie felt her face becoming warm and quickly looked down. "I've very much enjoyed making your acquaintance," she responded, keeping her hands busy unwrapping the bandage, hoping he wouldn't notice her fingers tremble.

"That's not much encouragement for a man who sits

waiting for your visits each day, but I'll not ask for more right now. Be prepared, however. Once I'm up and about, I plan to pursue you with vigor, doctor," his words carrying a fervor of determination.

"Let's just concentrate on getting you well for now," she replied, completing her ministrations and closing her black bag.

"If that's what the doctor orders, I'll agree for now," he responded, quickly placing a kiss on her fingertips before she could object.

"Edward!"

"Sorry, I'll try to keep myself under control," he replied, an unmistakable twinkle in his eyes.

"I must be going. I'll see you tomorrow afternoon. You may tell Mrs. Winter you have permission to be up in a chair for two hours each morning and afternoon and one hour in the evening if she can make arrangements to have you moved about," Tessie formally instructed.

"Yes, ma'am!" he replied, mimicking her formality.

"Have a good evening, Edward," she replied, unable to keep from smiling at his antics.

"It would be better if you'd return and read to me, but I suppose I'll have to make due with Mrs. Winter," he announced.

"You've convinced her to read to you?" Tessie asked, astounded by the remark.

"Of course. Since the first night I arrived," he told his incredulous visitor. "If you'd spend more time with me, you too would come to know just what a charming fellow I am."

"I don't doubt your charm, Edward. It's caused me enough problems already," she remarked, pulling on her gloves.

"Speaking of problems, you might put Mr. Banion on notice that unless he's managed to put a ring on your left finger by the time I'm out of this room, he's going to have some stiff competition for your affection," he stated, giving her a knowing wink.

"We'll see, Edward, we'll see," she replied, picking up her bag and leaving the room.

"Don't hesitate to come back after dinner," he called after her, as she walked down the hallway, a smile on her face.

She nearly collided with Mrs. Winter who was turning the corner, carrying a huge dinner tray.

"Just taking Mr. Buford his meal," she told Tessie. "Isn't he the most delightful gentleman? If I were thirty years younger, I'd set my cap for him," she announced.

"Mrs. Winter, you're a married woman," Tessie chastened.

"Nope. My husband's been dead over thirty years. He died a year after we were married. I wouldn't be working at this job if I had a husband, Dr. Wilshire, and if you're smart you'll find you a husband before you're too old! I thought I had time before I married again and decided I'd work awhile, spread my wings, but time got away from me. Before I knew it, I was too old and set in my ways to think about marrying again. Mark my words, you'll be sorry. Doctor or not, you'd better think about a husband," she earnestly counseled.

"Thank you for those words of concern, Mrs. Winter. I've given Mr. Buford instructions regarding his care and he'll relate those to you," Tessie stated, changing the subject. "If you can make arrangements for men to assist with moving him, I know he would be most appreciative. I must be going now," she continued, making a quick turn toward the kitchen to find Addie.

The two of them hurried home and Tessie had just finished washing the dinner dishes when Charlie knocked on the front door. Fatigued, Tessie had hoped he wouldn't return this evening and felt guilty when she opened the door only to be greeted by a huge bouquet of flowers.

"I hope you'll accept these with my deepest apologies," Charlie said, as he extended the bouquet to her and entered the house.

"Thank you, but flowers weren't necessary. Let me take your coat," she offered, as Addie came running across the room and wrapped her arms around his legs in a hug.

Charlie dropped to one knee and placed a kiss on her cheek. "Thank you for such a wonderful welcome," he said, squeezing her in return.

Tessie placed the flowers in a cut glass vase and turned toward Charlie. "Exactly what are you apologizing for?" she inquired.

"Whatever it is that made you angry," he responded.

"There! You see, Charlie, you don't even know what you've done to upset me. How can you apologize when you don't even recognize the problem?" she asked, her voice becoming incensed.

"I didn't come here to argue, Tessie. I came to apologize and try to forget what happened earlier today," he answered, not sure why she was becoming indignant.

Sensing things were not going well and in a childlike effort to calm the two adults, Addie pulled on Charlie's hand. "Tessie's going to get me operated on so I can hear again."

Charlie's mouth dropped open as he stared down at the child. "What? What is she talking about, Tessie? Did she say you're going to operate on her so she can hear again?"

"No. I'm not going to perform the surgery. We're not even sure about this yet so it's probably not worth discussing at this time. Why don't you sit down and I'll make some coffee," Tessie answered, not wanting to discuss the surgical plans.

"Don't bother with the coffee, I had some before I came. Why don't we all sit down," he said, his voice taking a note of authority. Clasping Addie's hand, Charlie led her to the couch where the child snuggled close beside him. Tessie would have preferred Addie go back to her sewing, but the child now seemed determined to insert herself in the middle of the discussion.

"About the flowers," Tessie began as she seated herself in the chair across from Charlie and Addie.

"Forget the flowers! What's this about Addie having an operation? When did all of this come about and why have I not heard anything? You'd think I were a stranger rather than a friend," Charlie stated, the hurt coming through in his voice.

Addie moved away from his side and was intently watching as he spoke, not wanting to miss anything he said. Her eyes darted toward Tessie and she realized her attempt to distract the couple from their earlier argument had been a failure. It appeared they were going to quarrel about the operation. Disconsolate, she settled back on the couch as Tessie leaned forward in her chair.

"Don't try to make me feel guilty because I'm attempting to find help for Addie. It's not as though I've been planning this for a long time. I was given information just yesterday regarding surgery that could possibly restore her hearing. The details are unknown to me as yet and I shouldn't have mentioned it to Addie until I knew more. I was so excited I couldn't help myself," she explained.

"You didn't seem to have any trouble keeping it from me," he bantered.

"I believe the majority of the time we've been together since you came to call at noon has been consumed with arguing," she retorted.

"Or the silent treatment," he shot back. "I'm sorry. That was uncalled for. I don't want to ruin the rest of the evening. Please tell me about this surgery. How did you find out about it?" he inquired, hoping the discussion about Addie would calm their nerves.

Tessie hesitated momentarily and then burst forth, "Edward's brother-in-law is a surgeon in Chicago. He went to Europe to study the technique and has successfully performed the surgery several times. His daughter is deaf, or she was before the surgery," Tessie hastily explained.

"Edward. I should have known," he said quietly. He felt as though his world was crashing in around him. Everything revolved around Edward.

Nobody said a word. Addie leaned her head against Charlie's arm. "I love you, Charlie," the child said, looking up at him.

"And I love you, sweet Addie," he said, giving her a hug. He could see the pain in Addie's eyes and resolved not to make matters worse.

"So what do you know of this surgery and this surgeon except that he's Edward's brother-in-law?" he inquired.

"Not too much. I've sent a letter to him today requesting additional information. I don't know if he'll even agree to see Addie, or if she would be a candidate for the operation. I'm hopeful I'll hear from him soon," she responded.

"So that was the rush to see Edward at noon and get to the post office," he surmised.

"Yes. He told me last evening about his brother-in-law

and the fact that his niece had been totally deaf prior to the surgery. He agreed to send a letter of introduction along with my inquiry to his brother-in-law. I wanted to get the letter posted as soon as possible," she stated.

"And what do you think about all of this, Addie? Are you excited about having an operation and perhaps being able to hear again?" he asked.

She shrugged her shoulders, a sorrowful look on her face. "I'd rather have you and Tessie be happy," she responded, causing the two adults to feel ashamed of their behavior.

"Perhaps we can do that," Charlie answered. "If we try real hard, maybe we can convince Tessie to go bowling and then get some hot chocolate. What do you think?" he asked.

"Oh, yes," she said, clapping her hands and looking at Tessie expectantly.

There was no way Tessie could refuse and Charlie knew it. It appeared he was going to have to use every tool at his disposal if he was going to outmaneuver Edward Buford—and he certainly planned to do that!

❧

With each passing day, Tessie would vacillate while walking to the post office. She wanted to receive a letter from Dr. Lundstrom, yet she feared what the contents would say. It was apparent he had received her letter because a wheelchair had arrived by train for Edward last week. As she and Addie made their way down the snow-covered sidewalk, she convinced herself Dr. Lundstrom did not want to see them and rather than write a letter of rejection, he was not going to respond.

Entering the post office, Jed Smith called out that she had some mail from Chicago and she felt her heart begin to race. Grasping Addie's hand, she quickly moved to where he stood and extended her hand.

"It's here someplace; saw it just a minute ago," he told her as he slowly checked through a stack of mail.

Attempting to keep her patience, she watched him slowly go through the pile, letter by letter, all the while wanting to grab it from him and find the dispatch for herself. *Be patient,* she kept telling herself as she waited, exasperation building with each moment.

"Ah, here it is," he finally stated, pulling out a cream-colored envelope. "Looks like it's from a Dr. Lundstrom," he said, reading the envelope before handing it to her.

Once home, she quickly pulled off her wraps and sat down in a chair close to the fire. Finishing the letter, she glanced toward Addie who stood staring at her, still bundled in her coat and muff.

"He wants to meet with us, Addie," she said holding her arms out to the child.

"Does that mean I'm going to have the operation?" Addie asked.

"Dr. Lundstrom said if we will come to Chicago he will examine you to see if the surgery would be helpful. If so, he is willing to operate," she told the child. "It will be wonderful, Addie. We'll have a nice trip and maybe you'll come back to Kansas able to hear again," she said, her voice full of encouragement.

"But what about Christmas? Will we have to leave before Christmas?" Addie asked. "Charlie promised we would all go to Christmas Eve services at church and that he would spend Christmas with us," she reminded.

"No, we won't go before Christmas. We'll wait until after the holidays," Tessie promised the child, but inwardly wished they could leave tomorrow.

Her last patient seen, Tessie bundled Addie in her warmest coat and the two of them made their way to the

Harvey House. Addie was off to the kitchen for John's beloved company, and Tessie rushed to Edward's room, anxious for his magnanimous encouragement.

"I've wonderful news," she burst out upon entering the room. Edward sat in the wheelchair staring out the window at a group of young boys playing in the snow. Her appearance brought an immediate smile to his face.

"You've heard from Byron?" he asked.

"How did you know?"

"Just a guess. I don't know too many other things that would cause you to burst into my room without a knock," he said, his voice filled with laughter.

"Oh, I'm sorry, Edward. I didn't knock, did I?" Her cheeks now flushed by her own embarrassment as well as the chill winds.

"I was only jesting with you, dear Tessie. You needn't become unduly distressed with your behavior," he advised, holding out his hand to her.

"Are you going to permit me to read the letter?" he inquired when she merely looked at his extended arm.

"Of course, I'm sorry," she apologized, flustered she hadn't immediately realized he wanted to read the correspondence.

"Tessie, you've done nothing but apologize to me since you entered the room. I must bring out your most conciliatory behavior," he stated with a smile as she pulled the letter from her handbag.

While Edward began to read, she removed her coat and hat, pulled off her gloves, and sat down in the rocker, watching his reaction as he read the letter.

"Well, it sounds very promising, don't you think?" he asked.

"Oh, yes. I'm delighted with the prospects," she told

him, leaning forward in the chair.

Grasping both of her hands in his he looked deep into her eyes. "This is going to work out wonderfully, my dear. When are you planning on going to Chicago?"

"I'm not sure, exactly," she stammered. "It's not that I wouldn't prefer to leave immediately, but Addie is looking forward to Christmas. I don't think we could possibly leave until after the holidays," she stated, careful not to explain Addie's desire to spend Christmas with Charlie.

"Oh," he responded in a disheartened tone.

"Why? What's the matter, Edward?"

"My sister and Byron would like for me to return to Chicago until I'm able to travel back to England. With the wheelchair, there's no reason why I can't take the train without fear of injuring my leg. I've told them I'd return," he explained.

"I see. Well, that certainly makes sense. There's no reason you should be sitting around in this hotel when you can be enjoying the company of your family while you recuperate," she concurred, when what she really wanted to tell him was not to leave, that she would miss him and needed him to stay and be her ally.

"So you want me to go?" he asked, hoping she would reject the idea.

"I didn't say I wanted you to go. I said it was a sensible plan," she responded.

"Do you want me to stay?" he asked, hopeful she would give the answer he wanted to hear.

"Your decision should not be based upon what I want. If you wish to travel to Chicago, it will not have an ill effect upon your recovery and you would, most likely, be more comfortable with your family. If, however, you desire to remain in Kansas until you've further recuperated, that would be wonderful. . .medically sound, that is," she stammered.

"I see. Well, then, how medically sound would it be if I remained in Kansas until you and Addie leave for Chicago and we make the trip together?" he questioned, a glint in his eye.

"I would say that would be very, very medically sound," she answered, thrilled that he would remain and travel with her, rather than enjoying the festivities with his family.

"Then that's what we'll do," he quickly responded, not wanting her to change her mind.

Suddenly, she felt ashamed of herself. Here was Edward, cooped up in his room except for his trips to the dining room and occasional visits with other visitors in the hotel, and she was encouraging him to miss the warmth and love of his family during their holiday celebration.

"I'm sorry, Edward. I'm acting very selfish. We both know the best thing for you would be to return to Chicago now so that you may be with your family. If you stay here, they'll miss the pleasure of your company through the holidays and you'll be stuck away in this room for Christmas, wishing you were there," she told him.

"They've done without the pleasure of my company for the holidays in years past, so I believe they'll survive without me again. As for being stuck away in my room, I'm sure we can find a couple fellows who would be willing to transport me to the home of one Dr. Tessie Wilshire for Christmas day festivities," he responded.

"Yes—of course—that could be arranged," she hesitantly replied.

"You could put a little more enthusiasm into that," he encouraged, giving her a bright smile.

"Oh, I'm sorry. Of course you're welcome to come and

spend the day with us," she stated, attempting to sound more zealous.

"That's more like it! We'll have a wonderful time," he told her.

"Well, well. Look at the time. I need to be getting home," she said, gathering her belongings.

"I'm so pleased this is going to work out, Tessie. We'll have a wonderful Christmas and the trip will be a grand adventure for the three of us," he concluded.

"Yes, I'm sure it will be a grand adventure," she said, forcing a smile. "I'll be by to check on you tomorrow. Good night, Edward."

"Good night, Tessie. I'll be busy making plans for Christmas," he said, giving her a cheerful wave.

Her head was whirring as she stopped by the kitchen for Addie. She didn't even hear John talking to her until he walked over and asked if she was ill.

"No, no, I'm fine, we just need to be getting home," she told the chef as she hurried Addie along.

The walk home was a blur. Neither of them spoke but Addie sensed something was very wrong. Tessie had been with Mr. Buford and now she was unhappy. It seemed to Addie that Mr. Buford was the center of the difficulty. She was beginning to dislike him and the problems he seemed to create.

"What's the matter?" the child asked while they were sitting at the dinner table. She had watched Tessie pushing her food around, not eating or talking.

"Nothing for you to be concerned about. I'm just trying to figure out a few things," she answered, realizing Addie had sensed her distress. "Everything's going to be fine," she stated, a little too brightly.

Addie protested going to bed, but Tessie held firm. She

needed time to think clearly and make some decisions about the approaching holiday. How was she going to handle both Charlie and Edward? There had been no way to avoid Edward's request to spend Christmas with them and yet Charlie had been invited weeks ago. Addie would never forgive her if she tried to exclude Charlie at this late date. She knew the day would be a disaster with both of them in the house, and was sure that nothing short of a miracle was going to prevent the day from turning into a donnybrook.

What have I done? she thought, drifting into a restless sleep fraught with bad dreams.

nine

Tessie eyed the letter on her bedside table. Slowly she removed the pages and began to once again read the latest missile from Dr. Lundstrom. He had solidified their travel plans, forwarded a plethora of information relating to the possible surgery. Additionally, he expressed his gratitude for her continued medical treatment of his brother-in-law, causing her a twinge of guilt.

"If it weren't for Edward, I'd probably have foregone this whole idea," she mused, certain she would have succumbed to Charlie's objections to the surgery. His negative responses and continual efforts to dissuade her had been the cause of many arguments. Edward, however, continued to encourage and bolster her pursuit, winning allegiance at every opportunity and becoming her sole confidant.

Tessie thought about the closeness she and Charlie once enjoyed, feeling the void of his lost companionship. She missed the ability to share things with him, but now was careful to tell him nothing of consequence. If he questioned, she adroitly changed the subject. Though she hadn't told an out-and-out lie, it was becoming increasingly difficult to feel at peace with this new behavior.

Guilt invaded her thoughts as she remembered her conversation with Edward earlier that day. Charlie would be furious if he knew the substance of that discussion, but she could think of no other solution to ensure Christmas wouldn't end in total disaster. Divulging her fear that the two men would misbehave, Tessie was aghast when Edward admitted such a prospect appeared uproariously inviting. It wasn't until she was reduced to tears he understood the depth of her anxiety over the ensuing holiday. Quickly he realized the situation could be used to his advantage. If he behaved according to her wishes, she would be eternally grateful. Especially if Charlie's behavior was dreadful—and he would certainly do all he could to help in that regard!

Miraculously, Tessie had convinced Uncle Jon and Aunt Phiney to bring the twins and spend the holiday in Florence with them. It had taken a good deal of persuasion since they were just as determined she and Addie should travel to Council Grove for the holidays. They finally conceded when she wrote explaining the possibility of traveling to Chicago for Addie's surgery immediately after Christmas.

It would be wonderful to have them visit and Tessie was sure they would help buffer the situation between Charlie and Edward. Addie's excitement that the twins would be coming with Uncle Jon and Aunt Phiney was evident. Tessie continued to remind her the twins were fourteen, but Addie was sure age didn't matter much on Christmas. It would be fun having other young people for the holiday.

❧

Charlie rushed to complete the last of his paperwork, anxious to be on the train headed for Florence and a week of vacation. The train pulled into the station just as he was putting on his woolen overcoat. Boarding the train, he leaned back and unbuttoned his coat, finally able to relax a bit. Surrounding him were gaily wrapped packages tucked into large brown bags, evidence of his shopping trip to Kansas City earlier in the month. Smiling, he realized it had been many years since the excitement of the holidays had affected him. It would be wonderful to see "his women" and share a magnificent holiday, certain they would be delighted with the many plans he had made for them.

The train pulled into the station exactly on time. Charlie quickly gathered the packages and swung down from the train, impatient to check into the Harvey House. It had been several weeks since he had seen Tessie, and although she seemed distant during his last visit, he was sure it was because they had both been so busy. Now they would have a full week to regain what seemed to be slipping away.

"Looks like Santa's already arrived," said Mrs. Winter as she walked to the front desk of the hotel and surveyed the profusion of packages.

"Not quite, but he's got a good start on things," Charlie stated with a laugh, pulling his arms out of his overcoat.

"I've got your room ready, just like you asked," she told him. "Just sign the register. You know the way," she told him, pleased to have Charlie as a guest. "John asked if you'd be having dinner with us tonight," she stated, with a question in her voice.

"Not sure, yet. Need to check with Tessie and see what she's got on her agenda," he responded.

"You just missed her. She was in checking on Mr. Buford," the matron informed him.

The comment hit like a jab in the stomach. *Why does she still need to visit Edward so frequently?* he wondered. Doctor or not, surely her daily presence wasn't still necessary. *Stop,* he thought, *or you're going to ruin everything before you even see her.* Picking up the packages, he went to his room, dropped off his belongings, and immediately left the hotel. Abandoning all thoughts of Edward, he attempted to regain the happy spirit he had felt before Mrs. Winter mentioned Tessie's earlier visit.

The walk to the house was invigorating. The cold air and dusting of snow gave the whole countryside a

Christmas card appearance. Knocking on the door Charlie stood patiently waiting, his breath puffing small billowy clouds of air in front of him.

"Charlie!" Tessie greeted, standing and staring from the doorway, her surprise unmistakable.

"Are you going to invite me in?" he asked, when she neither moved nor said anything further.

"Oh, yes, of course, I'm sorry," she responded, moving aside. "Come in."

"Charlie, Charlie!" Addie called, running toward him at full tilt, throwing her arms open for a hug.

"Hi, sweet Addie," he responded, picking her up into his arms and giving her a kiss.

"I've missed you, Charlie," she told him as he placed her back on her feet.

"I've missed you too, Addie, both of you," he said, glancing up toward Tessie, who appeared much less enthusiastic about his appearance.

"How about dinner with my two favorite gals at the Harvey House?" he asked.

"Oh, I've already begun dinner," Tessie quickly answered.

"Stay and eat with us, Charlie. Pleeeaze!" Addie begged, looking back and forth between the two adults.

"If it's okay with Tessie," he told her, wanting to stay, yet unsure from Tessie's behavior if she would extend the invitation.

"What can I say? Of course, please have dinner with us," she responded, walking back toward the kitchen.

"If I didn't know better, I'd think you weren't expecting me," he called after her.

The remark brought her back into the parlor. "I wasn't expecting you," she stated, looking at him as if he had lost his senses.

"Didn't you get my letter?"

"No, Charlie, I didn't receive a letter and I've been to pick up my mail regularly," she replied.

"I sent a letter with Harry Oglesby. We were both in Kansas City to meet with Mr. Vance. When I mentioned I needed to send you a letter, he said he had deliver it since he was passing through Florence. We agreed he would pass it along to Mary, my secretary, with instructions to deliver it to you right away. That was four days ago," he explained.

"I've never seen the letter, so perhaps you can enlighten me as to the contents while I finish preparing dinner," she requested.

Following her into the kitchen, he divulged the contents of his letter, wondering if Mary had received the letter from Oglesby. Tessie stood with her back to him as he excitedly related his plan to spend a full week in Florence.

"You're going to be here seven days?" she asked incredulously.

"Yes, isn't it wonderful? Wait 'til I tell you and Addie all the things I've got planned. I know a place not far from here where we can find a wonderful Christmas tree. We'll make it a real adventure for Addie. You know, find the perfect tree to cut down and decorate. Do you have any ornaments or shall we make some?" he asked, his enthusiasm overflowing.

"I have some ornaments, but I hadn't intended for you to plan our Christmas," she replied, watching her words immediately deflate his mood.

"I'm sorry. It's just that I've been going over all these ideas and my excitement has grown with each passing day. I thought it might be difficult for Addie since it will be her first Christmas without her mother and not having any word from Lydia. Anyway, I guess I got carried away thinking about how to make it special—for all of us," he finished, the enthusiasm gone from his voice.

Perceiving the obvious sadness caused by her biting remarks, Tessie felt a stab of remorse. If she didn't quit acting like such a shrew, Christmas would be spoiled for all of them.

"I'm sorry, Charlie, but you've caught me by surprise. It was extremely kind of you to think of Addie, but please understand that I've made plans too. When I didn't hear from you, I wasn't sure if you'd be here any longer than Christmas Day, if that," she told him.

"I promised Addie I would be here. Surely you knew I wouldn't break that promise," he said, wondering how they could have drifted so far apart in such a short time.

"Yes, I knew you'd do everything in your power to keep your promise," she agreed, placing dinner on the table.

"You say grace, Charlie," Addie instructed as they scooted their chairs under the table.

"I'd be happy to," he replied, looking at Tessie for an indication she was in agreement.

When she nodded her head he reached out and grasped one of Tessie's hands in his and Addie's in the other. He smiled as Addie quickly extended her other hand toward Tessie. With hands joined and heads bowed, Charlie gave thanks for their meal and asked God to direct them as they sought the best way to honor Him during the upcoming holiday celebrating the birth of His Son.

Charlie's simple request confronted Tessie with the fact that she hadn't been seeking God's guidance lately but just as quickly she brushed away the thought and began worrying how much she should tell Charlie about her plans.

"Guess what!" Addie exclaimed, before she had eaten her first bite.

"What?" Charlie asked, pleased with the child's exuberance.

Tessie moved to the edge of her chair, not sure what morsel of information Addie was going to offer.

"Uncle Jon, Aunt Phiney, and the twins are coming to see us. They're coming on the train the day before Christmas," she excitedly informed him. "Won't that be fun?"

"That's wonderful. It's nice to have lots of family with you for the holidays," he agreed, looking toward Tessie for confirmation that her family would be arriving.

"It took a bit of coaxing, but Uncle Jon finally relented. He was holding out, sure I'd come home for Christmas," she told Charlie.

"How did you convince them?" Charlie inquired.

Addie, who had been intently watching their conversation, answered before Tessie had a chance. "She told them I was going to Chicago for my operation right after Christmas, so they said they'd come here," she informed Charlie, proud she had been able to follow their conversation and now interject a meaningful piece of information.

Charlie's fork fell and struck the edge of his plate, a small chip of blue china breaking off and landing near the edge of the table. His head jerked up, a startled look on his face.

"What's she talking about? You haven't made definite plans, have you?" he asked.

"Yes, but I'd rather not discuss them right now. I know you don't agree with me about the surgery, but a discussion right now will only result in an argument. Let's try to avoid that, if we can," she requested.

"That makes it convenient for you, doesn't it? You tell yourself that keeping secrets and telling me half-truths is acceptable because you want harmony," he said, his voice calm, his face showing no evidence of anger.

"I want to spend a peaceful holiday. Is that so wrong?" she shot back.

"No, it's wonderful, but your actions belie what you say," he answered.

"And just what is that supposed to mean?" she asked, an edge to her voice.

"If you truly wanted a peaceful holiday, it seems you would have been open and honest in your actions. Instead, it appears you've been less than forthright and now plan to continue on that path using harmony as an excuse for your behavior. I don't plan to argue with you and I won't spoil this holiday. I may not always agree with you, but I've always treated you honorably. I wish you'd do the same for me. If you've been seeking God's will and He has given you direction, then I must believe your decision is for the best. As I continue praying about Addie's surgery, perhaps I'll develop a little of your assurance," he told her quietly.

Addie had been watching the exchange between the two people she loved most. She had understood most of what Charlie had told Tessie. She was glad he wasn't angry, but neither of them seemed happy, either. She moved from her chair, took hold of Charlie's hand and joined it with Tessie's.

"There!" she said. "That's better," and gave them a big smile.

How could they resist her simple solution? "We'll talk tomorrow," Tessie told Charlie. "Let's finish dinner."

When Charlie arrived the next day, Tessie kept herself busy with patients while Charlie entertained Addie. He'd brought a gift for them, one for before Christmas, he declared, and insisted Addie open it immediately. It was a beautiful nativity he had found at a tiny shop in Kansas City. They'd spent their time arranging the figures and later when Tessie peeked into the parlor she had heard Charlie telling Addie the story of Christ's birth. Addie watched his lips, intent on each word. As he explained about each of the characters, Addie would point to a figure, watching for his confirmation that she had understood. Tessie forced herself to move back into her office. Leaning against the side of her desk, she reminded herself that she needed to remember Charlie was her adversary when it came to Addie's surgery.

After lunch he asked if they could go looking for a tree. He explained he had made arrangements for a wagon and since her relatives would be arriving the next day, it would be the perfect time. She conceded Addie could go along but no amount of cajoling from either of them could cause her to give in and join them. Charlie was disappointed and Addie was confused by Tessie's attitude, but the two of them bundled up and had a wonderful time. They returned with one beautiful tree and four very cold feet several hours later.

Their discussion after dinner lasted much longer than either of them planned. Addie sat quilting, ignoring their conversation, and finally went to her room as one question led to another. Although Charlie was good to his word and didn't start an argument, he voiced his disagreement and unhappiness at some of Tessie's conclusions. He was hurt to find Edward had become her confidant. She immediately became defensive and wary during his questioning regarding the amount of time she had consumed seeking God's will for Addie.

"I've not been on my knees consistently, if that's what you're asking," she answered cautiously. "I did pray faithfully about Addie's hearing loss until Edward's appearance in Florence with news of the surgery. I feel that is God's answer," she replied, annoyed at herself for feeling so sensitive about the decision.

"God's answer for Addie, or an opportunity for you?" he

asked quietly.

"That's unfair, Charlie. You think my primary interest is medical erudition for me and not Addie's welfare, don't you?"

"To be honest, I'm not sure about your priorities, but I do want you to know I've been praying steadfastly about Addie and the surgery since the day I learned you were considering it," Charlie told her as he got up from his chair and moved toward the closet where his coat hung. "I can't say that God has given me an answer, but I can tell you I feel very uneasy about the situation. I know it's not my decision to make, but I hope you'll take time to talk to God before you go any further."

"Edward's appearance and the fact that his brother-in-law performs such specialized surgery is surely a sign that Addie is meant to have the operation," she stated, quickly defending her stance. "I've been praying about Addie's hearing since she came to live with me and I have every confidence that the surgery will be a success. The difference between us is that I'm not afraid to put my trust in medical science," she retorted, as Charlie buttoned his overcoat.

"Be careful where you place your trust, Tessie. There are a couple verses in Proverbs—Proverbs 3:5-6, if I remember correctly, that say, 'Trust in the Lord with all thine heart; and lean not unto thine own understanding. In all thy ways acknowledge Him and He shall direct thy paths.' You might want to spend a little time with God and see if He's the one directing your path to Chicago," he said, walking back to where she sat.

Even though she knew he was standing directly in front of her, Tessie didn't lift her eyes from the floor. She sat staring down at his black leather shoes, wanting to lash out in anger. She knew Charlie spoke the truth, but she wanted the surgery to be God's answer for Addie. She wanted it so much she was afraid to pray, fearful God would send an answer she didn't want to hear.

Charlie knelt down and took hold of her hands. When she still didn't meet his eyes, he placed a finger under her chin and lifted her head. When her eyes were level with his, he smiled gently and tucked a falling wisp of hair behind her ear. "I've loved you since that first day in the train station when you came for your interview. Did you know that?" he asked her.

"Don't, Charlie! It will only make matters worse," she replied, dropping her gaze back to the floor.

"I don't want you to think anything that has been said here tonight alters my love for you. I've come to think of you and Addie as my women and I want the very best for both of you. If you decide it's best to go to Chicago, I'll support you in that decision but please don't hide things from me," he requested.

"You've been very good to Addie—and to me, Charlie. I appreciate your concerns and since you've asked that I not hide anything, you should know that we'll be leaving for Chicago the day after Christmas. Edward will be traveling with Addie and me. His sister requested that he return to Chicago until he's fully recuperated. Since we were making the trip so soon after Christmas, Edward decided he would wait and travel with us," she stated, never once meeting his intent gray eyes.

"It appears that nothing I've said has meant much to you. I've declared my love and offered my support. I had hoped you would at least give my request to seek God's guidance some consideration, but it seems you're determined to follow your own path. It doesn't appear you need me for anything. I'm sure Edward will provide delightful company on the trip. I hope you'll forgive me but I don't think I'll stick around for Christmas. Seems to me I make you uncomfortable and just between the two of us, Edward makes me uncomfortable," he said, rising and walking to the front door.

"Addie will be disappointed if you're not here for Christmas. She's planning on Christmas Eve services at church," she told him.

"I'm sure you can explain my absence to Addie. You and Edward can take her to church on Christmas Eve," he responded, turning the knob on the front door.

"You really are welcome to spend Christmas with us," she said, walking toward him.

"I don't think it would be wise. I have some gifts for Addie. I'll have John bring them by the house," he replied, shoving his hand into his coat pocket, his fingers wrapping around the small square box nestled deep inside.

"That would be fine," she answered, not sure what else to say.

"I'll be praying for Addie—and for you," he told her, walking into the cold night air.

"Merry Christmas," she murmured, watching his tall figure disappear into the darkness.

ten

The train slowly hissed and belched its way out of the station, Addie and Tessie seated across the aisle from Edward. Addie carefully positioned herself near the window. Having concluded Edward was the cause of Charlie's disappearance, she decided to show her displeasure by avoiding contact with him. Edward was delighted with the seating arrangement, entertaining Tessie with animated conversation, intent on keeping her from having any regrets about the trip. Tessie dutifully assisted Edward as they changed trains, with Addie scurrying along behind, resenting the object of Tessie's attention. As they boarded their connecting train, Edward quickly showed his displeasure at being forced to sit several rows behind his traveling companions. The moment a gentlemen riding behind them left his seat, Edward hobbled up the aisle on his crutches and dropped into the seat directly behind them for the remainder of their journey. It was a long, tiresome trip for Addie, who was meticulously endeavoring to hide her fears from Tessie.

As they disembarked the train, Edward immediately spotted his brother-in-law. Waving to gain his attention, Dr. Lundstrom hastened toward them, explaining he had already made the necessary arrangements for Addie's admittance as a surgical patient pending his examination the next morning.

"My wife and I would like for you to stay with us during your stay in Chicago," he stated to Tessie.

"It's lovely of you to invite me, Dr. Lundstrom, but I feel

127

it would be best if I remained at the hospital with Addie. She's going to be frightened and I don't want to cause her further distress by being unavailable," she explained.

"We have an excellent nursing staff and I'm sure her every need will be met," Dr. Lundstrom assured his visiting colleague.

"I don't doubt the staff's competency, but I won't change my mind about remaining at the hospital with Addie," she responded.

"As you wish. We'll make arrangements for another bed to be moved into her room," he conceded.

"I won't be long, Edward. If you think you'll be warm enough, why don't you just wait for me," Dr. Lundstrom suggested.

"I'll be fine," he answered, pulling Tessie toward him and kissing her thoroughly. "Byron will keep me informed on your progress, and I'll see you soon," he told her, as Dr. Lundstrom removed their luggage and came alongside to assist them from the carriage.

Addie attempted to digest the scene she had witnessed. What was that awful Edward doing kissing Tessie? Charlie wouldn't like it and she didn't either. She hoped Johnny would remember to give her letter to Charlie. Her shoes felt as though they were weighted with lead as they reached the front door of the building looming in front of them. It was bigger than any place she had ever been and reminded her of stories she had heard about dark ugly places where they kept children who had no parents. Walking through the door and down the shiny hallway toward a large oak desk, they stopped while Tessie signed papers and then the nurse escorted them into a sparsely furnished room.

After bidding Dr. Lundstrom farewell, the two of them unpacked some of their belongings, grateful for something to pass the time.

"Do you think it would be all right if I put it on the bed? Will they get angry?" Addie asked, pulling her recently completed quilt from one of their bags.

"I don't think anyone will mind but if they do, they'll have to take it up with me," Tessie responded, posing with fists doubled and arms lifted in a boxing position. Addie laughed at the sight and the two of them placed her beautiful quilt over the starched white hospital linens.

Settled in her room several hours later, Addie watched as Tessie sat writing a letter. "Are you writing to Charlie?" she inquired, carefully tucking the quilt around her legs.

"No, I'm writing to Uncle Jon and Aunt Phiney. I promised to let them know we arrived safely," she replied, noting Addie's look of disappointment to the response. "I'm not going to send it until after Dr. Lundstrom's examination in the morning. That way I can tell them what he has to say about your operation."

"I think I'll go to sleep. Want to say prayers with me?"

"I would love to pray with you, Addie," Tessie replied, moving to sit on the edge of the bed.

Addie's prayer was simple. She thanked God for everything, requested she not die in surgery because she wanted to be at Charlie and Tessie's wedding, and told Him it would be okay if she couldn't hear after the operation since she was doing all right since she had been living with Tessie.

Tessie leaned down to kiss her good night, hoping Addie couldn't see the tears she was holding back. She sat watching the child long after she had gone to sleep, wondering if she really didn't care if the operation was successful. *Is she subjecting herself to this ordeal merely to please me?* she mused and then pushed the thought aside, sure that the statement was merely a protection mechanism the child was using in case the surgery failed.

Morning dawned and the sun shone through the frost on the window, casting prisms of light on the shiny hospital floor. Dr. Lundstrom strolled into the room, his shadow breaking the fragile pattern. A nurse in a crisp uniform followed close at his heels.

"Good morning. I trust you two women slept well," he greeted.

"As well as can be expected in a hospital room far from home," Tessie replied, giving him a bright smile and taking hold of Addie's hand, in an attempt to relieve any developing fear.

Looking Addie squarely in the eyes, his lips carefully forming each word, he smiled and said, "I have a daughter two years older than you. She was deaf also, but now she can hear. I hope I will be able to do the same thing for you. If we can't perform the surgery or if it isn't successful, I hope you will learn to sign. It will make it much easier for you, especially to receive an education. Now, let's get started with the examination."

Tessie realized his words were meant for everyone and without further encouragement moved away from the bed. Quickly the nurse moved into position, anticipating Dr. Lundstrom's every request. Addie remained calm and cooperative throughout the probing and discussion, her eyes fixed on an unknown object each time the doctor turned her head in yet another position.

"Thank you, Addie, for being such a good girl," Dr. Lundstrom told the child as he finished the examination. "I'm going to talk with Dr. Wilshire and then we will decide what's to be done."

As if on cue, the nurse left the room as quickly as if she had been ordered. "Would you prefer to talk here or in an office down the hall?" Dr. Lundstrom inquired.

"Right here would be fine. I don't want to leave Addie,"

she explained, turning to face him as he pulled a chair alongside her.

"I hope you don't feel I was rude by not including you in the examination. Being emotionally involved with a patient can sometimes cloud our vision. I speak from experience. If you elect to move forward with Addie's surgery, I will include you completely if that's your desire."

"Does that mean she's a good candidate for surgery?" Tessie inquired, unable to contain her excitement.

"It means I will consider surgery. It's difficult to know what caused Addie's deafness. I'm guessing from what you told me in your letters that she was slowly losing her hearing. Being a child, she probably didn't realize it was happening and that she should be hearing more competently. I imagine it went unnoticed by her mother and sister until she was nearly deaf. The procedure I perform, if successful, would restore her hearing by probing the cochlea and allowing sound to pass directly into the inner ear."

"Your diagnosis is that the stapes has become immobile, is that correct?"

"I'm impressed, Dr. Wilshire. You've either been doing extensive research on your own or had excellent medical training."

"Both," Tessie replied. "As a matter of fact, I took my medical training right here in Chicago, but I've been reading everything I could obtain since Edward told me of your surgical procedure."

"You must understand that even if the surgery is successful, Addie's hearing won't be completely normal and there will most likely be some hearing loss after the operation. With the sound bypassing the entire chain of bones in the middle ear, it is impossible for hearing to be completely normal. You must also be aware that for several days, sometimes even weeks, a patient can suffer from severe vertigo. I need not tell you what a dreadful experience that can be. After three days of suffering with dizziness and nausea, my daughter wasn't sure the cure was worse than the affliction."

"She has no regrets now, does she?" Tessie asked, sure of what the answer would be.

"No, she has no regrets. Nor do we. You can't, however, base your decision on our circumstances. I don't envy you in your decision. It's a difficult decision when all the facts and circumstances are known. In Addie's case, we're groping for background information and merely able to make an educated guess. Even though you're a physician and have researched hearing impairments, I'm obligated to advise you there are other risks with the surgery."

"Yes, I realize there are risks," Tessie interrupted, "but if there's any possibility for Addie to regain her hearing, I think we should proceed with the surgery."

"Please let me finish, doctor."

"I'm sorry," Tessie apologized, feeling the heat rise in her cheeks.

"As I was saying, along with the normal risks related to surgery, there is the possibility of infectious bacteria infiltrating the inner ear which can be deadly. I've already advised you of the probability of vertigo. Additionally, it can be psychologically devastating for the patient when they awaken and can hear the sounds around them and after a few hours they are once again deaf. Although it hasn't happened in any of my surgeries, there is the possibility the operation will be a complete failure and she might not even have the opportunity to hear for a few hours. This is not a decision to be made lightly, but should you decide upon surgery, I would be willing to perform the operation. Why don't you and Addie take the rest of the day to decide and I'll stop back this evening."

"When would you perform the operation—if we decide to go ahead?" Tessie inquired.

"I think it would be best to wait a few days. You are both tired and I'll want additional time to examine and observe Addie," Dr. Lundstrom replied, sure the young doctor had made up her mind to proceed with surgery before ever setting foot on the train from Kansas. "Would you like to assist, or at least observe—if you decide to go ahead?"

"Oh, yes," Tessie responded, her heart racing with excitement over the thought of assisting in such an innovative operation.

"Which?" he inquired.

"Assist, by all means, assist," she state emphatically, giving him the answer he expected before he had ever posed the question.

"I'll leave the two of you to make your decision," he replied, walking to Addie's bedside. Taking her hand in his he looked into the deep brown eyes that stared back at him. "It's been nice to meet you, Addie, and if you decide to have the operation, I hope I'll be able to help you hear again."

"I'll have the operation. That's what Tessie wants," she candidly responded in a soft voice.

"What about you? Don't you want to hear again?"

"I suppose but it doesn't seem as important as it used to."

"Why is that?" he asked, sitting on the edge of her bed.

"I wanted to hear again because I thought I wanted to be a doctor like Tessie."

"Has something changed your mind about wanting to be a doctor?" he inquired, encouraging her to continue with her thoughts.

"I'd still like to be a doctor, but this trip to Chicago and the operation made Charlie unhappy. Now he and Tessie are angry. I miss Charlie and want things back the way they were—even if I can't hear," she responded in a sorrowful voice.

Glancing over at Tessie, he wondered if the child's words would cause her to have second thoughts, but quickly realized they would not. Her resolve was obvious; she had decided Addie needed the surgery and surgery she would have.

He smiled down at the child, remembering the turmoil of making the same decision for his daughter. He hoped things would turn out as well for this little girl with a pretty quilt tucked under her chin.

"Just where did you get that beautiful quilt?" he asked. "I know that's not hospital fare."

"Tessie and I made it," the child proudly responded.

"She did most of the work," Tessie quickly interjected, "and has become quite a little seamstress in the process."

"Tessie has her own quilt that she made. It's bigger than mine," Addie continued. "Tessie told me her quilt was sewn with threads of love. Mine has woven threads, three of them, to sew the binding, see?" she told the doctor, holding the quilt up for his inspection.

"That's very pretty, was it your idea?"

"No, Aunt Phiney suggested it. When she was with us for Christmas she told me quilts are special in our family. She said the woven thread I used weaves me into the family," the child proudly related.

"What an exceptional idea," the doctor responded, touched by the child's seriousness.

"She's a wonderful child, isn't she?" Tessie queried, noting the doctor's look of amazement at Addie's answer.

"That she is, and then some. . . ," he replied.

"Charlie! Hold up, Charlie, I've got a letter for you," John Willoughby called out to the figure rushing into the train station.

"What are you doing in Topeka, John?" Charlie inquired, startled to see the chef from the Florence Harvey House running toward him.

"Keeping a promise to a little girl," he responded, bending forward against the cold blast of air that whipped toward him. "Let's get inside before we both freeze to death," he said, pushing Charlie inside the door. "I don't know about you, but I'm heading straight for a hot cup of coffee. Care to join me?"

"I guess if I'm going to find out what you're talking about, I'd better," Charlie answered, tagging along behind. "What's this all about?" he asked, after they'd removed their coats and settled at the lunch counter.

Reaching into his jacket pocket, John retrieved an envelope and handed it to his friend. "Addie made me promise I'd get this letter to you. I could have taken a chance on mailing it or having someone else bring it, but I promised Addie I'd deliver it by today. So, here I am. Don't let me stop you, go ahead and read it," he encouraged.

Charlie stared down at the sealed envelope, his name printed in a childish scrawl across the front. A tiny heart drawn in each corner. He tore open the envelope, unfolded the letter and began to read. When he had finished, he carefully folded the letter, returned it to the envelope and took a sip of the steaming coffee sitting on the counter.

"I don't know what to do, John," he said, looking down into his cup. "Addie's asked that I come to Chicago to be with them. I feel terrible, she's almost begging."

"Well, what's stopping you? Catch the next train and go be with them," John responded, wondering why someone as bright as Charlie Banion couldn't figure that out on his own.

"You don't understand. Tessie and I had quite a disagreement about the trip to Chicago. I'm not convinced she should be rushing Addie into this operation and I told her so. Needless to say, that didn't sit too well with her."

"Hmmm. I suppose that does muddy up the waters a bit, but I think that little gal needs you there right about now. Maybe you two adults need to put aside your own feelings for the time being, and concentrate on Addie," he said, rising from the counter and slipping his arms into the wool overcoat. "I'm going to get me a room and then head back to Florence in the morning. I know you'll do what's right, Charlie."

"Thanks for bringing the letter so quickly, Johnny," Charlie called to the bundled-up figure.

Johnny turned and looked at Charlie, saying nothing for a brief moment. Slowly he walked back to the lunch counter. "I think a lot of that child too, Charlie. I felt honored she trusted me enough to ask for my help. I'm just praying everything turns out okay for her. Gotta go," he said, his voice beginning to falter.

Charlie watched the door close and soon felt the blast of cold air that had been permitted entry. A quick chill ran up his spine. *I'll accomplish nothing, sitting here,* he thought, pulling on his coat. Heading toward the station to check train departures and connections that would get him to Chicago, he jotted down the information and then began the chilling walk to the boardinghouse he called home when he was in Topeka.

After what seemed like hours of prayer, Charlie fell into a restless sleep. He awoke the next morning feeling as though he had never been to bed, still not sure what he should do. "Lord, I hope there's an answer coming soon, because that little girl's going to have her operation soon and I don't know what to do," he said, looking into the mirror as he shaved his face.

"There's a telegram from Mr. Vance on your desk," Mary called to him as he brushed by her desk and into his office. Charlie didn't acknowledge her remark, but she knew he had heard.

"He's sure been in a foul mood lately," Mary whispered to Cora. "He pays even less attention to me now than he used to. One of the waitresses over at the Harvey House told me he had his cap set for that redheaded doctor. You know, the snooty one that came here and interviewed," she explained as Cora took a bite out of a biscuit smeared with apple butter.

"I know who you're talking about, Mary. I was here when all that happened!"

"I know, I'm sorry, but it's hard for me to understand. The waitress said Dr. Wilshire had given him the glove, so you'd think he would show a little more interest in me now. Wouldn't you?" she asked imploringly.

"Who knows what men want," Cora answered. "I'm sure no authority, but it's not as if you don't have plenty of fellows interested in you. Why don't you just give it up, Mary? Sometimes I think you like the chase. Once you've snagged someone, you're not interested anymore," her friend remarked, wiping her lips.

"I supposed there is some truth in that," Mary sheepishly replied. "I'll just ignore him, maybe that will get his attention!"

Cora shook her head at the remark. Mary hadn't listened to a word she had said.

"Mary, bring your notebook in, I have a few things that need to be completed before I leave for Chicago," Charlie called.

Giving Cora a wink, Mary seated herself across from Charlie without uttering a word.

"I'll be leaving for Chicago later this morning, Mary. Mr. Vance has called a meeting of company officials and since he is in Chicago at the present time, he's requested we come there. I'll wire you information on how you can reach me in event of an emergency. I don't know when I'll be returning, but I'll wire that information once I'm sure of a date. Now, let's get some letters taken care of as quickly as possible. I need to be ready to leave on the 11:00 A.M. train and I'll need to get home and pack my things," he advised, and quickly began dictating the first of several letters.

Rushing to board the train, Charlie knew his answer had come. Mr. Vance wanted him in Chicago, Addie wanted him in Chicago, he wanted to be in Chicago, and he now felt certain God wanted him in Chicago. He wasn't quite so sure about Tessie, but he was positive Edward wanted him anywhere but Chicago. Leaning back in his seat, he hoped the trip would pass quickly and he would reach the hospital in time to be of comfort to Addie.

eleven

Hearing Dr. Lundstrom's voice in the hallway, Tessie looked up to see the doctor walking toward their room with an attractive young woman at his side. "Tessie, Addie, this is Marie. She works at our house and very much enjoys being with children. She spends a good deal of time with Genevive, our daughter, and would like to stay with Addie so you can join us for dinner this evening. I will not take 'no' for an answer. Marie understands deaf children. Addie will be in very competent hands. Marie will not leave her side, and you need to have some time away from here. It's going to be a couple of days before surgery and then the recuperation period afterward. It's necessary for you to get out of the hospital at every opportunity to revitalize yourself," he said, walking to the small closet and removing Tessie's coat.

"I don't think it would be a good idea to leave," she stammered, looking at Addie who was already being entertained by Marie.

Tessie walked over to Addie. "Do you mind if I leave for a while?" she asked. Addie shook her head giving permission, then quickly returned to the game she and Marie were playing.

"I guess I've been dismissed," she said to Dr. Lundstrom, slipping her arms into the wool coat he held out for her.

"You'd better get your scarf and gloves. It's very cold," he instructed, as the two of them waved to Addie and Marie.

"We met Marie on one of our trips to Europe. She was

employed at one of the hotels where we stayed. None of her family is alive. Genevive took a shine to her and Marie was able to communicate and entertain her like no one else except my wife. Since she needed a home, and we needed assistance with Genevive, it turned out to be an excellent arrangement for all of us. She quickly became part of the family. Genevive adores her, thinks of her as an older sister, I believe. When Marie discovered you were here alone, she offered to make herself available so you could have some respite during Addie's hospitalization. We've agreed it would be a wonderful arrangement for all of you. Now that Genevive can hear again, she's not nearly as dependent upon Marie. Nowadays, Marie has turned into my wife's social secretary and confidant. I don't think she enjoys it nearly as much as being with children," he said, a smile breaking across his face.

"That is a most generous offer, Dr. Lundstrom. I don't know how frequently I will feel comfortable to leave Addie, but I assure you I am indebted to you and your family for the many kindnesses you've extended us," she responded as their carriage turned into an oval driveway and stopped in front of an exquisite brick mansion.

"We're here," he said, assisting her from the carriage. "Edward will be so delighted. He has been after me to bring him to the hospital, but with this cold, snowy weather, I thought it better he stay indoors. If I hadn't returned with you, I think he would have walked to the hospital. He is quite taken with you, but I'm sure you know that," he told her, as they entered the front door.

"Tessie, I can't tell you how grand it is to see you," Edward said, swinging toward her on his crutches and quickly placing a kiss on her cheek.

"Edward, please don't be so forward," she rebuked.

"We're all family here, Tessie. They don't mind a bit.

No one would know how to behave if I acted in a refined manner all the time," he said grabbing her hand and placing a kiss on her palm.

"You must be the incredible Dr. Tessie Wilshire I've been hearing so much about. I'm Juliette Lundstrom, Edward's sister," said the striking brunette who came gliding toward Tessie, her hands outstretched in welcome. "We are so pleased to have you join us. I hope it will be the first of many visits," she continued, leading the group into the dining room.

Hours later, Tessie was startled when she glanced at the hand-carved clock sitting on the mantle. "I didn't realize it was so late. I must get back immediately," she said, quickly rising from her chair. "Addie probably thinks I've deserted her. Juliette, may I have my coat, please," she requested.

"If I know Marie, Addie is probably fast asleep, having had a most enjoyable time this evening," Juliette responded. "I do understand your concern, however. I'll only be a minute and we'll get you back to the hospital."

Byron and Juliette bid her good night and allowed Edward a few minutes of privacy as he escorted Tessie to the door. "I want you to promise you'll come back tomorrow evening," Edward cajoled. "I'm not allowing you to leave until I have your word," he stated emphatically.

"I don't know, Edward. I really need to be spending my time with Addie."

"Tell me you haven't enjoyed the adult companionship and some decent food? Tell me it hasn't refreshed you to be away for a few hours? I'm going to expect you here tomorrow evening. Edward's carriage will bring Marie and fetch you back. I know Addie won't care a bit. There's not a child who doesn't love to be with Marie. If Addie is completely unhappy with the arrangement, you send Marie back with the message and I'll force Byron to allow me a visit with you at the hospital. Do we have a bargain?" he pleaded.

"You are so difficult to refuse, Edward. I have enjoyed the evening. Your sister and niece are so lovely and, of course, you know how much I admire Byron. I guess we have a bargain," she responded, pulling on her gloves and looking up at him.

He seized the opportunity and leaned forward on his crutches, pulling her to him. "Don't back away, my love, or I'll fall on the floor," he whispered in her ear, embracing her. "Oh, Tessie, I've missed you so," he murmured.

"Edward," she began, bending back to meet his eyes, but was stopped short as he quickly lowered his head, placing a lingering kiss on her partially open lips. "Edward, you must stop or I will leave you lying flat on the floor," she breathlessly chastised him. He smiled, gave her one more fleeting kiss, and backed away, knowing his kiss had left its mark.

"Ah, Tessie, you are the woman of my dreams," he told her. "And I intend to have you!"

"I think I'll have some say in the matter," she replied, as he opened the front door.

"That you will, that you will," he retorted. "See you tomorrow evening and thank you for coming," he called after her.

❧

Juliette had been right. Addie was fast asleep and Marie was busy with her embroidery when Tessie returned to the hospital. Addie's exuberance the next day assuaged any feelings of guilt Tessie had about returning to the Lundstrom's for dinner again that evening. In fact, Addie encouraged her to go. Marie had promised to bring a new game for them to play and it was obvious she was looking forward to spending more time with the young woman.

"You're sure you don't mind?" Tessie asked for the third time as Marie came walking down the hallway of the hospital.

"No, go," Addie answered. "Marie and I will have fun," she answered, just as Marie entered the room carrying a satchel that immediately caught Addie's attention.

Several hours later a noise in the hallway caused Marie to look up. Standing in the doorway was a tall, handsome man, a valise in one hand and a gaily wrapped package in the other.

"Charlie," came the resounding call from Addie. "Oh, Charlie, you came to be with me," the child cried, bounding into his arms.

"And who might you be?" Charlie inquired, looking directly at Marie, noting she was the only other person in the room.

"I'm Marie, an employee of Dr. Lundstrom and his wife," she replied. "Who are you?" she asked, although it was obvious Addie knew this man well.

"Charlie Banion. A friend of Addie's. Where might Dr. Wilshire be?" he asked, hoping she would pleased to see him.

"She's gone to the Lundstroms for dinner. Dr. Lundstrom thought she needed some relaxation away from the hospital and, of course, Edward has driven everyone mad since Dr. Lundstrom wouldn't allow him to leave the house and visit Dr. Wilshire here at the hospital. He's truly smitten with her and I can certainly understand why. So beautiful and such a fine woman," she confided, not realizing the impact her words were having upon Charlie.

"Yes, she is beautiful," Charlie answered. "You know, I'd really like to spend some time alone with Addie and I'm sure you wouldn't mind having some extra time for yourself. I'll take over your duties here and you can go ahead and return home," his voice carrying enough authority that Marie knew she had been dismissed.

≈

"Marie, what are you doing home?" Dr. Lundstrom called from the dining room, as the young woman entered. Tessie immediately rose from her chair, concern etched on her face.

"Sit down, Dr. Wilshire. Everything is fine. A friend of Addie's is staying with her. She assured me you wouldn't mind a bit. It appeared they wanted to visit privately, and he bid me leave them."

"He? Did you get his name?" Tessie asked, still alarmed at the turn of events.

"Oh, of course. Mrs. Lundstrom would have my hide for such an omission," she answered, giving her mistress a smile. "His name is Charlie Banion. A fine looking man, I might add. Will you be needing me for anything further this evening, Mrs. Lundstrom?"

"No, nothing else, Marie. Thank you," Juliette responded, noting their guest had turned ghostly pale.

"I really must return to the hospital," Tessie stated, again rising from her chair.

"But you haven't eaten. Sit down and finish your meal. I'll have the driver return you immediately after dinner," Dr. Lundstrom ordered.

She certainly didn't want to insult the doctor. Even though she knew staying was a mistake, she couldn't afford to offend him. After all, he would be operating on Addie soon. Slowly she sat down and finished the longest meal of her life, dreading the meeting she would soon have with Charlie, knowing what he must be thinking when she didn't immediately return.

≈

Hearing the click of shoes coming down the hallway, Charlie glanced at his pocket watch. It was almost 8:30 P.M. He was sure it must be Tessie. When she hadn't returned shortly after Marie left, he knew she was sending him a message, a message he didn't want to receive. His heart skipped a beat as she entered the room, her cheeks flushed from the cold, even more beautiful than he remembered. He had vowed to keep things civil—not lose his temper. The last thing he wanted was to drive her further into Edward's arms.

"Tessie, it's good to see you," he welcomed, rising from the chair beside Addie's bed. "You look wonderful."

"What are you doing here, Charlie?" Her voice wavered between hostility and dismay.

"Why don't you take off your coat and I'll explain," he answered warmly, although his first thought had been to ask where she had been when he arrived at the hospital.

"Don't fight, please don't fight," came Addie's plea from the bed, causing Tessie to feel ashamed of the way she had greeted Charlie. "I love both of you and I want you both with me," Addie continued. "So, just talk nice and love each other," the child instructed.

"We'll try our best," Charlie answered, giving her a wink. "Why don't we sit down over here. Maybe Addie will be able to get to sleep and won't be able to read our lips quite as easily."

"Folks are missing you in Florence," he began. "Doc Rayburn can't wait for you to return. Says he doesn't know how you ever talked him into coming out of retirement during your absence. And the folks at church, they've all been praying for you and Addie," he continued.

"I'm pleased to hear that, Charlie," she interrupted, "but what I really want to know is why you're in Chicago. You're opposed to all of this and then, without a word, you show up like you belong here."

"I do belong here, Tessie. Addie had John deliver a letter to me asking that I come to Chicago. I have prayed earnestly about this operation and what my role should be. I know we differ about the surgery, but I hope we both want what is best for Addie, not ourselves. I had just about decided to make the trip and then I got a wire from Mr. Vance calling a meeting here in Chicago. So, you see, I had to come to Chicago. I guess some folks would say it was Mr. Vance that called me here. I think God called me here," he finished.

"And me, too. I called you too," Addie stated, from across the room.

"Addie, how were you able to read my lips from over there?" Charlie asked, moving toward her.

"I didn't," she answered. "I listened with my ears."

"What are you telling me? Are you saying you can hear like you used to?" he asked.

"Almost. It's just a little quieter, but it's louder today than yesterday," she responded with a bright smile.

"Addie, why didn't you tell me?" Tessie inquired incredulously.

"Because I knew you wanted to learn all the operation. I heard you tell Dr. Lundstrom today how excited you were about helping with my operation and that it was a big opportunity. I didn't want to spoil it for you," she answered soulfully.

"Oh, Addie. What I wanted was for you to be able to hear again and instead I've made you feel that all I was interested in was learning a new surgical technique. Perhaps I was thinking more about myself than you," she answered, tears welling in her eyes.

"Don't cry, Tessie. I wouldn't have let you do the operation. I heard Dr. Lundstrom reminding you about that dizzy stuff I'd have after the surgery. If it hadn't been for that, I might have let you do it, but I don't want to be woozy and throwing up for days," she stated.

Long after Addie had fallen asleep, Tessie wrestled with herself. Before Charlie left for his hotel, the three of them had joined in a prayer of thanks for Addie's restored hearing, but she knew Addie had spoken the truth. The surgery had become an obsession and she didn't want anyone or anything attempting to dissuade her. She wanted her way in the matter, not Addie's and certainly not God's. Completely ashamed of herself, she knelt down beside her bed and earnestly prayed for God's forgiveness. Forgiveness for her self-serving attitude after He had entrusted her with the care of this young child, and forgiveness for the way she had treated those who questioned her decision, especially Charlie. Climbing back into bed, she fell into a deep restful sleep, the best she had had since meeting Edward Buford.

૨૪

"No one knows exactly what causes things like this to happen," Dr. Lundstrom stated to Tessie. "My guess is that some severe trauma in her life caused her hearing loss. I don't know if it was the fear of surgery that caused her hearing restoration or not," he continued.

"No, it was God. I'm really sure it was," Addie interjected to the group of adults gathered in her room.

"I vote with Addie," Charlie stated.

"And so do I," Tessie remarked.

"Edward asked that you come by the house as soon as possible. He'd like to visit with you. I know you're planning on leaving in the morning so I told him I'd bring you home with me," Dr. Lundstrom told Tessie.

"I have a meeting to attend, so I must be on my way," Charlie stated. "Addie, I'll see you as soon as my meeting is completed," he told the child and walked toward the door.

"I'll see you later too, Charlie," Tessie called after him.

Several hours later Charlie returned. Pulling Addie's coat from the closet, he told her she was certainly well enough to go out for lunch with him. Over the nurse's protest, the two of them met Mr. Vance for an elegant meal in one of the fashionable downtown restaurants. Addie charmed both of them throughout the meal, and profusely thanked Mr. Vance for allowing her to come along to such a fancy place. As they were leaving, Addie told Mr. Vance it was nice to meet him and then stated, "You must come to Florence sometime. Our lunch today was very good. But my Johnny's food at the Harvey House is even better." Both men appreciated her remark, knowing she probably spoke the truth.

Tessie was waiting in the hospital room when they returned and Addie quickly related all the details of the fancy luncheon she had attended. "How was Mr. Vance?" Tessie inquired.

"He's doing just fine. He asked I send his regrets that you hadn't been available to have lunch with us. And your meeting with Edward, how did that go?" he inquired, knowing he might be overstepping his bounds.

"We can talk about that on the train ride back to Kansas. I assume you're leaving in the morning, also?" she inquired, not wanting Addie to be a part of their discussion about the meeting with Edward.

"Yes, in fact I was hoping you'd agree to leave the hospital now. We can get you and Addie registered at the hotel and at least have an enjoyable dinner together. That is, if you don't have other plans," he offered.

"No other plans. I think you've had a grand idea. It will be nice for Addie to see a little of Chicago. I know I'd sleep better in the hotel than this hospital and it would be fun to have dinner together again," she answered.

For the most part the trip home was pleasant, although they were all anxious to get back to Florence, making the journey seem longer than anticipated. Charlie proved to be a much more enjoyable traveling companion than Edward, showering attention on both Addie and Tessie. When Addie fell asleep on the seat in front of them, Tessie revealed to Charlie that Edward's intentions had been honorable. He proposed marriage and wanted her to move to Chicago. He had already discussed the matter with his brother-in-law and the two of them had agreed Tessie could join Byron's practice and work at the hospital with him. He wasn't as thrilled about the prospect of having Addie, however. His plans for her were a boarding school in England where she would attend classes and have occasional visits with them. It would be a much better life than anyone would have ever have anticipated for the "poor waif" he had explained to her.

"You know I would never do that to Addie, Charlie," Tessie said, watching as he bristled at the remarks.

"Yes, I know that. I also know you'd never let a man plan your life for you either. Apparently Edward didn't know quite as well as I do," he said, laughing at her look of mock indignation.

"I really am sorry for all the trouble and pain I've caused you, Charlie. I hope you'll forgive me. I know things can never be the same between us. I've ruined that with my lack of trust in you, but I hope you'll remain our friend," she implored.

"Tessie, I had hoped you knew my feelings for you were deeper than that. Surely you know I'll forgive you. I love you, and with that love comes my understanding and forgiveness. It may take a little time for us to get back to where we were, but I'm certain we will. Hopefully, even further," he said, leaning over to kiss her on the cheek.

"Thank you, Charlie," she whispered, slipping her hand into his.

❧

"Welcome back!" Johnny called out to the trio as they stepped down from the train. "I got your wire saying Addie was fine and you were coming home today. Told the kitchen help they'd better keep things on schedule 'cause I was coming to meet my friends."

"Johnny," Addie called, rushing to meet her favorite chef. "I can hear now, isn't it wonderful?"

"You bet it is, little woman. It's good to have you home, all of you," he answered, amazed with Addie's ability to once again hear. "Restores your faith, doesn't it?" he said, to the adults.

"It certainly does and then some," Tessie replied. Charlie gave her a knowing look and squeezed her hand, leading them into the station.

"Mary, get yourself over here and take a gander. Looks like Mr. Banion's back in the doctor's good graces again," Cora told her friend. Rushing forward, Mary peeked around Cora's plump figure.

"Wouldn't you just know it!" she seethed.

"I think you better give up on this one. It appears to me they're headed for the altar," Cora replied, sounding smug.

"Whose side are you on, anyway?" Mary asked, noting Cora's tone of voice.

"This time I think I'm on that little girl's side. They make a nice looking family, if you ask me and there's plenty of other men for you to conquer," her friend answered.

"Well, thanks for nothing," Mary replied, stomping back to her desk, while Cora stood watching the threesome gather their baggage and walk away from the station.

Tessie smiled down at Tessie as she tucked her into bed. "I'm glad we're back home," Addie said, after they had finished prayers.

"Me, too," Tessie and Charlie replied in unison, causing all three of them to laugh. "You get right to sleep, and tomorrow we'll talk about enrolling you in school. It's going to be such fun for you, new friends and I know you'll be an excellent student. I love you, Addie," Tessie lovingly told the child, leaning down to kiss her good night.

"I love you," the child answered, "and you too, Charlie," she said holding her arms open for a hug.

"I'll make some coffee," Tessie told Charlie as they exited the child's bedroom.

"Sounds great," he replied, walking toward the fireplace to jostle the logs, hopeful a little more heat would quickly be forthcoming. "Wish John had thought to get this place warmed up a bit before we returned," he called out toward the kitchen.

"John doesn't even have a key to the house, Charlie," she replied.

"If I'd have been thinking I would have wired him. Doc Rayburn could have let him in. Oh well, I didn't think of it, so we'll have to abide the chill for a bit."

"Maybe this will warm you up," Tessie said, handing him a hot cup of coffee.

Taking the cup, he patted the sofa cushion. "Sit down here, next to me," he instructed.

Obediently she seated herself and stared into the fire, her hands wrapped around the steaming cup of coffee. "It's so good to be home. It seems as though I've been gone for months instead of a few weeks," she said, still staring toward the fire.

"Tessie, if you're not too tired, I'd like to talk a little," Charlie stated, hoping she would allow him to continue.

"As long as I can just sit and listen. I'm not sure how much I'll add to the conversation," she replied, with a smile.

"I'll only expect a few words here and there," he responded. "On the train, when I told you I loved you, I meant that with all my heart. I also meant what I said about it taking us a little time to heal our wounds. What I would like is for you to accept this," he said, pulling a ring box from his pocket.

"Oh, Charlie," she stammered, "you told me I wouldn't have to think. . ."

"Let me finish. I purchased this ring for you before Christmas. Then with all the problems, I wasn't sure you'd ever agree to be my wife. I've kept it with me since the day I purchased it, hopeful one day you would accept it. I bought this ring for you. I want you to be my wife, but we need more time. All I'm asking is that you wear this ring as a symbol of our agreement to determine if we're truly meant for each other. If that doesn't happen, you may keep the ring—my gift to you. Although, I do feel reasonably certain I'll be placing a wedding band on your finger in the future. Can you agree to my proposal, Tessie?"

She nodded her agreement, holding out her left hand and watching as he slipped the ring on her finger.

"You've made me very happy, Tessie," he said, pulling her close and tenderly enfolding her in his arms. "I don't know what I would have done, had you not agreed."

The mantel clock struck nine, just as he rose from the sofa. "I think, perhaps, I'd better get back over the Harvey House and make sure they haven't given my room to some-one else. Besides, we both need some sleep," he said walking with her toward the door. "I'll see you in the morning," he called back as she stood in the doorway waving, cold air rushing into the entry.

❧

Two days later Charlie and Tessie enrolled Addie as Mrs. Landry's newest student at the small schoolhouse several blocks away. Throughout the day, Tessie found herself thinking of the child. In the midst of examining a patient or cleaning her instruments, her mind would wander to Addie and how her day was going. Shortly before the school bell clanged announcing the end of the school day, Charlie arrived at the door.

"Wanted to be here and see how she made out," he told Tessie. "Think I'll wait out here on the porch."

"Charlie, it's cold," she protested.

"I know, but I want to see her face. I'll know how it went when I see her face," he replied.

Tessie smiled and grabbed her coat, pulled it tight around her and sat down in the other chair. "I hope she comes quickly," she told him with a grin.

No more had Tessie uttered the words than Addie came skipping down the sidewalk, a smile from ear to ear, holding the hand of another little girl. "Hi," she called out to the couple sitting on the porch "This is my new friend Ruth," she announced, pulling the youngster up the steps to meet Tessie and Charlie.

"I'd say things went well," Charlie whispered to Tessie and held out his hand to meet Addie's new friend.

❧

In the months that followed Tessie medical practice continued to grow, and Addie flourished in the new world unlocked to her. Their days were busy, but Charlie was still required to travel much of the time and both of them missed him.

It was an especially lovely spring day when Tessie

decided upon meeting Addie after school. Charlie was expected to arrive and they would walk over to the station and meet him.

"What a pleasant surprise," Charlie exclaimed, walking into the station, and gave Addie a big hug while kissing Tessie's cheek. "To what do I owe this unexpected event?"

"It's such a beautiful day, I met Addie after school. We thought it would be nice to greet you here at the station and walk to the house with you," she replied, pleased she had made the decision.

"Just let me drop my bag off with Mrs. Winter in the hotel and we can be on our way."

They walked slowly enjoying each other's company as well as the budding trees and flowers. "Is someone sitting on the porch?" Addie asked, squinting to get a better look.

"It does look like there's someone in one of the chairs," Charlie replied, as they continued moving toward the house.

"It appears to be a woman and baby. Probably someone with a sick child waiting to see me," Tessie stated, quickening her step.

"No," Addie said, coming to a halt. "It's Lydia."

"It is Lydia," Tessie answered, attempting to conceal her fear. "I wonder what she's doing in Florence," Tessie said, looking toward Charlie.

"Well, she does have a sister here," Charlie reminded her.

"Yes, I know, but she's been gone all this time without a word and now suddenly she appears on the front porch."

"Don't get alarmed. Let's just remain calm and welcome her," he said opening the gate, although he noted Addie hung behind, not overly anxious to see her sister.

"Bet you're surprised to see me," Lydia said rising from the chair and adjusting the small child on her hip. "This here's Floyd, Jr.," she announced to the three of them.

"Well, he certainly is a fine looking boy, isn't he?" Charlie observed, glancing at Tessie for confirmation.

"Yes, he is," Tessie replied. "How have you been Lydia?"

"Well, right now I'm hot and tired. Any chance I could get something to drink and maybe a bite to eat?" she inquired. "Hi, Addie," she said, to her sister without so much as a hug, brushing by her to follow Tessie into the house.

It was obvious Lydia wasn't going to divulge what was on her mind until she was good and ready. She had always been deceptive and although Tessie had been slow to learn that lesson, she was on guard. Quickly she prepared cold drinks and arranged some cookies and biscuits on a plate. Returning to the parlor, she found Charlie and Lydia engaged in polite conversation. Addie had disappeared from sight.

"Here you are, Lydia," Tessie stated, offering a glass of lemonade and the plate of cookies.

"I was hoping for something a little more substantial than cookies, but guess they'll do for now," she answered, quickly devouring several.

"So how are things going with you and Addie? Must be okay since you didn't put her in an orphanage or get rid of her," Lydia stated, slapping the baby's hand when he reached toward the plate of cookies. Tessie inwardly winced at the punishment.

"They're going fine, Lydia. I've grown to love Addie very much, she's like my own child. I've often wondered how things turned out for you and Floyd."

"Well, it ain't been no bed of roses, that's for sure. Floyd was gone all the time with his sales job and me, I was home alone with the baby. Then one day Floyd tells me he's met up with someone else and he's leaving me. I've been trying to make it on my own but with Floyd, Jr., but I just can't. That's why I'm here," she announced.

"Why?" Tessie asked, still unclear what the connection might be.

"Because I need someone to take care of Floyd, Jr., so I can work. I figured Addie ought to be good for that. If she watches him careful she could handle him, even if she is deaf. So, I came to take her off your hands," she stated, as if those were the words Tessie had been waiting to hear.

"Take her off my hands? What are you thinking, Lydia? I'm not going to allow you take Addie. It was you that made the decision to leave her, and here she'll stay," Tessie snapped in response.

"You've no right to her. She's my blood, my sister. If I say I'm taking her, that's how it will be and I don't think there's much you can do about it," Lydia retorted.

"Ladies, women," Charlie interrupted. "I think we all need to calm ourselves a bit. Lydia, I'm sure you're tired after your journey from—where did you come from Lydia?"

"From Kansas City, and I used about all my money just getting here," she answered.

"Whereabouts in Kansas City?" Charlie questioned. "I've spent quite a bit of time in Kansas City myself."

"Not where we were living, I'm sure," she replied, going into detail about the row of shacks where they lived along the riverfront. Charlie listened intently, and questioned her for details she seemed pleased to pass along, wanting all of them to know the poverty in which she had been forced to live.

"Well, I'm sure you and Floyd, Jr., are both tired. Why don't I take you down to the Harvey House and get you a room. There's plenty of time to discuss this tomorrow after you've had a good night of rest," he counseled.

"I'm not going to change my mind about this no matter if

we discuss it now or in the morning. Besides, I can't spare the money for a hotel room," she said, looking around the house as though the accommodations there would be just fine.

"Well, I'll be more than happy to pay for your room, Lydia," Charlie offered. "I'll talk with Mrs. Winter and have it put it on my bill, your meals too. That way you don't have to worry," he said, leading her toward the front door.

"Mrs. Winter? Is that old fuddy-duddy still around? Are any of the women I worked with still there?" she inquired excitedly, never giving another thought to Tessie or Addie.

"Is she gone?" Addie asked, peeking around the corner.

"Yes, for the moment anyway," Tessie responded. Addie flew into her arms and clung for dear life.

"You won't let her take me, will you?" the child tearfully questioned. "I don't want to go with her. She doesn't care about me, she just wants me to watch her baby. I don't know anything about taking care of babies, do I?" she asked, hoping that particular fact would change the situation.

"I don't want you to worry about this, Addie. Charlie is coming back and we're going to find a way to work things out. Charlie always has good ideas and I'm sure he'll think of some way to convince Lydia you should stay with me," she soothingly answered, just as Charlie entered the front door.

"Did you get her settled?"

"I'm not sure settled is the word," he answered. "I got her a room, but she found a couple of the waitresses she had worked with before. When I left she was busy drinking coffee and visiting with them. I'm afraid poor Floyd, Jr., is in for a night of it. She'll probably keep him up until all hours while she gossips with the women."

"Tessie said you always have good ideas and that you'll

figure out a plan so Lydia will go away. You can do that, can't you, Charlie?" Addie interrupted, her voice trembling.

"Addie, I can't promise to make Lydia leave, but I'll do everything I can possibly think of to keep you with Tessie—and me," he added. "I think it might be better if we cancel our plans for dinner at the Harvey House this evening. How about going to the cafe downtown? They have some pretty good food, too."

"I think that's an excellent idea," Tessie responded and Addie shook her head affirmatively.

&

After Addie had gone to bed, Tessie and Charlie sat on the front porch, wanting to be sure she didn't overhear their conversation, something they were having to get used to. It occurred to Tessie they hadn't even told Lydia that Addie's hearing had been restored—not that Lydia would have particularly cared unless it was of benefit to her.

"We're going to have to handle this very carefully, Tessie. I understand your anger and your fear because I have those same feelings, but Lydia isn't going to back down just because we tell her. I'd like to get this resolved as quickly and painlessly as possible, but I'm afraid if I offer her a sum of money, she'll keep coming back for more. I think we must come up with a permanent solution that will benefit her, Floyd, Jr, and the three of us, especially Addie."

"I agree with everything you've said, although I do have trouble holding my temper. Her audacity truly offends me, thinking she can just waltz back into Addie's life and turn it upside down whenever it suits her fancy. Have you thought of a plan that she might agree too?" Tessie questioned, trying to calm herself.

"I have an idea she's not been entirely truthful with us and we'll need time to verify what she's told us. It's going to be difficult to placate her if she becomes suspicious, but in order to discover the truth, I'm going to have to leave town. In the morning I'll tell Lydia that I must leave town on business, which is true enough, and request she wait until I return to make a final decision regarding Addie."

"Do you really think she'll agree to that?" Tessie inquired.

"If I offer to pay the tab for her little vacation at the Harvey House, I think she'll agree. We may have to offer babysitting services if she wants to go out partying with her friends," he said, giving her a lopsided smile.

"I'd keep him the whole time you're gone if it would help. Speaking of which, how long do you think you'll be gone?" Tessie asked.

"If everything goes as planned I should be back in two or three days at the most, but in the event this fails, we'll have to come up with an alternate plan. You might give that some consideration and prayer while I'm gone. I hope you trust me to handle this," he stated.

"I trust you implicitly, Charlie," she answered.

"In that case, I think it's about time we added a wedding band to that engagement ring," he said with a wink. "Perhaps you could spend a little time making wedding plans, too?" he continued, with a question in his voice.

"Perhaps I could," she answered, looking into his gray eyes.

Gently he pulled her to him and slowly lowered his head. "I love you, Tessie Wilshire," he said and then gently kissed her. "I'll stop by tomorrow after I've talked to Lydia, but for now I'd better get back over to the hotel," he said, walking toward the door.

Encircling her in his arms, he smiled down at her. "We'll see this through, Tessie. Things will work out, you'll see," he said, kissing her gently on the lips.

"I know you're right. I'll try to quit worrying and start praying," she responded, hoping God would lead Charlie in the right direction.

"Good! I'll see you sometime tomorrow morning," he replied. "Now, I'd really better be on my way."

Tessie watched as he walked toward the Harvey House. *He is truly a marvelous man. How did I ever consider anyone else?* she thought to herself.

The next morning Charlie arrived shortly after ten o'clock. "Things are looking like they might work out. I've convinced Lydia to sit tight as my guest at the hotel and she seems willing to do that. She was complaining about the baby and I told her if she needed a brief respite, you would most likely agree to care for him so long as it didn't interfere with office hours," he said, almost apologetically.

"Charlie, that's fine. I said I didn't mind, and I don't. It's the very least I can do while you're off tracking down information," she told him.

"My train leaves in an half an hour so I can't stay, but if Lydia attempts to take Addie, rely upon John for assistance. I've filled him in and he said he'll keep an eye on her over at the hotel. He'll have no problem getting information from the waitresses about what Lydia's telling them."

"I'm glad you thought of John as a resource. He's been a trusted friend and Addie loves him so much. I know he had do anything to help her," she stated, pleased to know she would have an ally while Charlie was gone.

"It seems all I do is leave you, but I must get over to the station," he said.

She reached up and placed her hands on either side of his face. "I love you, Charlie Banion," she sighed.

"You're not making it any easier for me to leave," he said, leaning down and ardently kissing her. Quickly, he moved away. "If I don't make an exit now, I may never go," he told her and bounded down the steps, with a wave.

Lydia lost little time making her way back to visit Tessie,

causing Addie to hide in her room immediately upon her sister's arrival. "This kid is drivin' me crazy," she stated, plopping Floyd, Jr., on the floor. "Mr. Banion said you'd watch after him while he was gone, so I brought his clothes and things," she said, dropping a satchel beside the baby.

"Lydia, Mr. Banion told you I would watch the baby so long as it didn't interfere with my office hours. I have patients to see and certainly can't watch your baby. If you want to go somewhere this evening with your friends, bring him back then," Tessie said, trying to keep her voice friendly.

"I guess if I can't leave him, I'll have to take Addie over to the hotel with me so she can watch after him. I'm planning on enjoying this little holiday," she stated in a menacing voice. "I think I've got the trump card, Doctor Wilshire. What's it gonna be, Addie at the hotel or Floyd, Jr., at your house?"

"Floyd, Jr., at my house," Tessie answered. "You certainly seem to have no qualms about disposing of the people in your life, do you Lydia?"

"Nobody ever had much problem disposing of me, either," she angrily retorted. "Are you keeping him or not?"

"I said I would. When will you be back?"

"Mr. Banion said he had be gone a couple days. Guess I'll be back when he is," she retorted and walked out slamming the door behind her, frightening Floyd, Jr., who began to wail. Addie, who had been listening to the conversation, came running out in need of consolation just as a patient walked into the office. Tessie wasn't sure where to turn first.

Tessie took them both into the office with her and within a short time Addie had become fond of the baby and was entertaining him. By the end of the day, he was in love with Addie and she was in love with him. He held his chubby arms out for Addie, not Tessie, and in no time she was diapering and feeding him as if she had been doing it all her life.

"Don't get too attached, Addie. Lydia will be back in no time and Floyd, Jr. will be gone. Enjoy him while you can, but remember he'll be leaving soon," she reminded the child, fearful the baby's departure would be difficult.

"I know, I know," Addie would answer and immediately begin hugging and kissing Floyd, Jr., who was thoroughly enjoying the continuous attention.

Two days later Charlie returned.

twelve

Addie peeked through the lace curtains, watching as Lydia sauntered toward the front door, a smug look on her face. "She's coming," the child called out in a hushed voice.

"It's all right," Tessie reassured. Floyd, Jr., was in Addie's arms, much cleaner than when he had arrived although his clothing was tattered and permanently stained from lack of care. *He is a sweet child,* Tessie thought, watching him play with Addie's hair.

Tessie opened the front door just as Lydia had raised her hand to knock. "Couldn't wait for me to get here, could you? Now you know how it feels, being tied down to a kid all the time," she greeted in a taunting voice.

"It's nice to see you, Lydia," Tessie responded, ignoring the hateful remark. "As soon as Charlie arrives we'll have dinner," she offered.

Lydia seated herself on the sofa and stared after Addie who was headed for the backyard carrying the baby. Tessie had expected the baby to miss his mother and show excitement at her reappearance, but that didn't occur. Floyd, Jr., clung to Addie who appeared to be his preference, at least for the time being. Lydia didn't seem to mind, however, showing no interest in either of the children.

"She seems different somehow. Probably 'cause she's living the good life here with you—but not for much longer. She'll soon remember what it's like to do without all this finery," Lydia stated smugly.

Tessie inwardly grimaced at the thought of Addie being required to live with Lydia. It was obvious she would be

163

reduced to servant status and once again become the brunt of Lydia's bitterness and resentment.

"Where is Mr. Banion, anyway? He told me to be here at five o'clock. I'm not waiting around forever. Maybe he ran out on you, just like Floyd did to me. Men have a way of doing that," Lydia retorted, above the rumbling of the evening train as it pulled into the station.

"I'll be just a few moments. I need to check things in the kitchen," Tessie replied, her palms wet with perspiration.

Where can he be? she thought, not sure how much longer Lydia would remain. She stood there envisioning Lydia grabbing Addie and whisking her off into the night, never to be seen again. *Stop this nonsense,* she admonished herself, quickly bowing her head in prayer to ask God's forgiveness for not trusting this matter to His care. "Father, I know there is no problem You can't handle, if we'll just remember to ask and place our trust in You. I'm doing that now, and will cease this useless worrying." No sooner had she uttered the prayer than the command in 1 Peter 5:7, came to mind, "Cast all your cares upon him; for he careth for you." An awareness of God's peace was now with her as she returned to the parlor.

Walking into the room, Tessie stood back as the front and back doors opened simultaneously. "Charlie, Floyd," came cries from the assembling group.

"What's he doing here?" Lydia fumed, pointing her finger in Floyd's direction. Floyd, Jr., began crying, wriggling in Addie's arms in an attempt to reach his father.

"Here, I'll take him, Addie. How's Daddy's boy?" Floyd crooned to his son. "How are you, Addie?" he asked, tousling her hair and giving her a genuine smile.

"I'm just fine, Floyd. I can hear again," Addie told him.

"Why that's wonder—"

"What do you mean, you can hear? Nobody told me

anything about you hearing? Were you just play acting for more attention, you little brat? You always got the best of everything, even now," the older sister enviously raved.

"Stop it, Lydia! Stop it, right now. Mr. Banion knows all about what's gone on between the two of us. I even told him about not wanting to leave Addie but that you insisted on running off, away from Florence, away from Addie, away from everything. Even when I offered to quit my sales job and stay in Florence so Addie could live with us, you wouldn't agree. You had to go to the big city. Well, you've been there, Lydia. Now, what? Are you going to ruin everyone else's life, deciding what you want next?"

"You know, I think it might be best if we all just relaxed a bit and had dinner. We can talk after we've eaten," Tessie suggested, not wanting a full-fledged battle to take place in front of the children.

"That's a good idea. I could eat a horse," Charlie replied.

"You could? Not me, I'd never eat a horse," Addie giggled back.

"You would if you were hungry enough," Lydia angrily shot back at the child.

Addie moved closer to Charlie, feeling the need of his protection against this woman who was so full of hate. Why did her sister despise her so, Addie wondered, as they sat down at the table.

Tessie's roasted chicken, creamed potatoes and peas, butterhorn rolls, and apple cobbler were eaten in formidable silence. Charlie and Tessie made feeble attempts at dinner conversation, only to be cut short by Lydia's caustic rebuttals. Floyd held the baby, spooning mashed potatoes into the child's mouth, unable to conceal his embarrassment.

None of them failed to note Floyd's compassionate nature with his son. Where Lydia slapped and hollered,

Floyd praised and coaxed. When Lydia was annoyed with the baby's antics, Floyd was delighted. It was obvious he loved his son and was obvious that Lydia had woven a tale of lies.

After dinner, Floyd, Jr., asleep in his father's lap and Addie in her bedroom, Lydia admitted Floyd had not run off and left her.

"But, why did you do this, Lydia? I just don't understand," Floyd questioned.

"I don't think you really want to know, Floyd."

"Yes, I do. How can we fix this unless I know what's going on?"

"I don't think you can fix it, Floyd, but here goes," she replied. "I can't stand being tied down to the baby all day. He gets on my nerves. You get to be gone, out seeing other people and come home and all you do is play with him. All I do is cook and clean. I want some fun out of life, Floyd. Can't you understand that?"

"If the baby is such a problem for you, why'd you bring him? Why didn't you just slip away at night and leave him with me? You could have left him, just like you left your sister," he retorted.

"To tell you the truth, I thought about that. Long and hard. But then I decided upon this plan, which would've worked if you hadn't gone and found him," she fumed at Charlie. "Speaking of which, just how did you know where to find Floyd?"

"You gave me enough information about where you lived that it didn't take much investigating to find him. All I had to do was ask a few people to do a little inquiring."

She glowered at him, hating his ability to out-smart her, ruining her plans.

"You still haven't told us about your great plan," Floyd insisted.

"Oh, what's the difference, I might as well tell you. Everything's spoiled now anyway. I figured if I said I was taking Addie and going to make her take care of Floyd, Jr. while I was working, Dr. Wilshire would offer me money so she could keep Addie. I wasn't gonna take the money right away. Thought I'd find someplace a ways off, over to Marion or Lost Springs and get a job. Make her real lonely for wonderful little Addie, until she offered me as much money as I wanted. Then I'd give her back, take Floyd, Jr. back to you and be off to make a life for myself. Not a bad plan until Mr. Banion stuck his nose in the middle of it."

"Lydia," Floyd whispered, "how could you ever think of doing something so cruel and mean-spirited to people who have loved you and tried to be kind?" he asked in disbelief. "I don't even know this person. . .this creature. . .who would plot to hurt others so ruthlessly, without a thought for them. Your own flesh and blood, Lydia, your sister, your own son, me, Dr. Wilshire, Mr. Banion, all people who have loved you or tried to help, and all you want to do is inflict pain on us. Why, Lydia, why?" A tear overflowed and rolled down his cheek.

"Stop it, Floyd. Quit acting like such a milk toast, crying like your kid. Why don't you grow up and see what life is really like, I've had to. I really got nothing more to say to any of you. Since you're so all-fired in love with that kid, you figure out how to take care of him and hold down a job. Me? I'm gonna start over and never look back. Don't any of you ever come looking for me, either. You're all a part of my life that never existed. My life's starting the minute I walk out this door," she replied, a loathing look aimed at all of them.

They watched as she rose from the chair and stormed out the front door, never giving a second look at her husband or child.

"What's gotten into her? I just don't understand," Floyd said to no one in particular.

"It's not what's gotten into her, Floyd, it's what hasn't. She's looking for good times and money to take care of filling the void in her life, but she'll find out it won't cure what ails her. The hole Lydia feels inside, that desperate longing to be accepted and loved, needs to be filled and only God can heal her. The pain will cling to her like an undesired affliction until she turns to the One Who loves her in spite of all her shortcomings," Tessie told him.

"What are you going to do, Floyd?" Addie asked. The adults wondered the same thing, but didn't broach the question.

"Right now I think the baby and I need to be with family until I get things sorted out. I think I'll head back to Ohio. I can stop in Kansas City and close out the apartment, then go see my folks. I'll leave my address with you and our landlord in Kansas City. In case Lydia decides she wants to come back, she'll need to know where to find us," he stated hopefully.

Charlie and Tessie agreed that Ohio sounded like a good place for a fresh start. His parents were still there to help with Floyd, Jr., and being settled in one place would allow him the opportunity to spend more time with his son.

"You're always welcome to come visit with us, Floyd," Tessie told the young man. "Addie has become very attached to Floyd, Jr. in the short time he's been here and I know she's going to miss him. We all will," she added.

"I'll keep in touch with you. I'm not real good at letter writing, but I'll try. You'll let me know if you hear from Lydia, won't you?" he asked.

"Of course, we will. If she contacts us, we'll be sure she receives your address," Tessie reassured him.

"Guess I better get over to the hotel. I need to make train

reservations and get some sleep before we leave in the morning. I really appreciate what you've all done for me and the baby. Especially you, Mr. Banion. If you hadn't come and found me, I hate to think of what Lydia might have done," he told them. "I'm sure glad you folks decided to keep Addie. She'll have a good life with you. Lydia would destroy her," he stated sadly, walking out the door.

The next morning, Tessie, Charlie, and Addie watched as Floyd boarded the train, the baby in his arms. He looked forlorn and dejected but his smile returned when he gazed down at his son. He kissed the baby's rosy cheek and whispered to him, "Who knows what will happen? Maybe one day God will open your mama's heart and she'll come back to us."

"I've made a decision." Charlie told his two favorite women as they walked home.

"What might that be?" Tessie asked.

"I think the three of us need to sit down and do some serious planning for a wedding. You two women aren't getting things moving toward the church quick enough to suit me," he stated with mock indignation.

"Charlie, it's only been a few days since you told me to start making plans and we have had a few major interruptions in our life," Tessie retorted.

"Don't worry, Charlie. Tessie's has her wedding gown ready to go. She had it even before you asked her to get married," Addie told him.

"Is that so? Pretty sure of yourself, were you?" he teased.

Tessie felt a blush rise in her cheeks. "It's not what you're thinking at all. One day when Addie and I were talking, I mentioned that when I got married I would wear my Aunt Phiney's wedding dress. So, you see, I wasn't being presumptuous," she told him, as they walked onto the porch and he leaned down to kiss her.

"You can be just as presumptuous as you like, Dr. Wilshire, as long as it's me you're marrying in that dress. So, when's the date? Have you talked to the preacher? What about a special dress for Addie? Shall be get married here in Florence or do you want to go home? How about a big cake, what do you think, Addie? A really, really big cake?" Charlie asked, clasping his outstretched hands and forming his arms into a huge circle.

Addie laughed at him, his good mood contagious. "We'll need to make another quilt," the child informed them.

"Why do we need another quilt?" Charlie inquired when Tessie nodded her head, agreeing with the child.

"So we can weave you into the family, just like me," Addie replied.

"I'm all for that, just as long as you wait until after the wedding to make it!" Charlie told the two of them.

"I think that's one thing that can wait," Tessie agreed.

"Well, this can't," he replied, pulling her into his arms and kissing her thoroughly while Addie sat on the front steps giggling, unable to conceal her happiness.

A Letter To Our Readers

Dear Reader:

In order that we might better contribute to your reading enjoyment, we would appreciate your taking a few minutes to respond to the following questions. When completed, please return to the following:

Rebecca Germany, Managing Editor
Heartsong Presents
P.O. Box 719
Uhrichsville, Ohio 44683

1. Did you enjoy reading *Woven Threads?*
   ❑ Very much. I would like to see more books
     by this author!
   ❑ Moderately
     I would have enjoyed it more if _____

     _____

2. Are you a member of **Heartsong Presents**? ❑Yes ❑No
   If no, where did you purchase this book?_____

   _____

3. What influenced your decision to purchase this
   book? (Check those that apply.)

   ❑ Cover   ❑ Back cover copy

   ❑ Title   ❑ Friends

   ❑ Publicity   ❑ Other_____

4. How would you rate, on a scale from 1 (poor) to 5
   (superior), the cover design?_____

5. On a scale from 1 (poor) to 10 (superior), please rate the following elements.

___Heroine   ___Plot

___Hero   ___Inspirational theme

___Setting   ___Secondary characters

6. What settings would you like to see covered in **Heartsong Presents** books?_____
_____
_____

7. What are some inspirational themes you would like to see treated in future books?_____
_____
_____

8. Would you be interested in reading other **Heartsong Presents** titles?   ❑ Yes   ❑ No

9. Please check your age range:
   ❑ Under 18   ❑ 18-24   ❑ 25-34
   ❑ 35-45   ❑ 46-55   ❑ Over 55

10. How many hours per week do you read? _____

Name _____

Occupation_____

Address _____

City_____ State_____Zip_____

LoveSong

Do you have a **Heartsong Presents** title that you can no longer find or a favorite that you would like to have in large print? Barbour Publishing announces six classic **Heartsong Presents** historical romances. . .now available in trade paper size.

____*Dakota Dawn* by Lauraine Snelling is the tale of a Norwegian immigrant and a North Dakota farmer whose ideal plans have been suddenly rearranged.

____*Eyes of the Heart* by Maryn Langer is about Prudence Beck who is alone in the logging country of Washington Territory and longs to make a life for her unborn child.

____*Heartbreak Trail* by VeraLee Wiggins follows Rachel's adventurous trip along the Oregon Trail, one that soon turns to sorrow.

____*A Light in the Window* by Janelle Jamison is the story of a nurse in the Alaskan wilderness whose career is threatened by a determined suitor and an outbreak of diphtheria.

____*Proper Intentions* by Dianne L. Christner is set in Ohio as the nineteenth century approaches and orphaned Kate longs for a husband and family of her own.

____*The Unfolding Heart* by JoAnn A. Grote shows what happens when a creature of comfort faces the crude and dangerous Minnesota frontier and discovers a strong love for a down-to-earth minister.

Send to: Heartsong Presents Reader's Service
P.O. Box 719
Uhrichsville, Ohio 44683

Please send me the titles checked above. I am enclosing **$3.97 each** (please add $1.00 to cover postage and handling per order. OH add 6.25% tax. NJ add 6% tax.). Send check or money order, no cash or C.O.D.s, please.

To place a credit card order, call 1-800-847-8270.

NAME _____

ADDRESS _____

CITY/STATE _____ ZIP _____

......Heart♥ng ......

HEARTSONG PRESENTS TITLES AVAILABLE NOW:

(If ordering from this page, please remember to include it with the order form.)

········ Presents ········

Great Inspirational Romance at a Great Price!

Heartsong Presents books are inspirational romances in contemporary and historical settings, designed to give you an enjoyable, spirit-lifting reading experience. You can choose wonderfully written titles from some of today's best authors like Peggy Darty, Sally Laity, Tracie J. Peterson, Colleen L. Reece, Lauraine Snelling, and many others.

When ordering quantities less than twelve, above titles are $2.95 each.
Not all titles may be available at time of order.

Hearts♥ng Presents
Love Stories Are Rated G!

That's for godly, gratifying, and of course, great! If you love a thrilling love story, but don't appreciate the sordidness of some popular paperback romances, **Heartsong Presents** is for you. In fact, **Heartsong Presents** is the *only inspirational romance book club*, the only one featuring love stories where Christian faith is the primary ingredient in a marriage relationship.

Sign up today to receive your first set of four, never before published Christian romances. Send no money now; you will receive a bill with the first shipment. You may cancel at any time without obligation, and if you aren't completely satisfied with any selection, you may return the books for an immediate refund!

Imagine. . .four new romances every four weeks—two historical, two contemporary—with men and women like you who long to meet the one God has chosen as the love of their lives. . .all for the low price of $9.97 postpaid.

To join, simply complete the coupon below and mail to the address provided. **Heartsong Presents** romances are rated G for another reason: They'll arrive *Godspeed!*